x

2-13

WAY
OF THE
OUTLAW

Center Point
Large Print

Also by Lauran Paine and available from
Center Point Large Print:

The Man Without a Gun
The Guns of Parral
The Gunsmith
Ute Peak Country
Way of the Outlaw
Beyond Fort Mims

WAY
OF THE
OUTLAW

— A Western Story —

LAURAN PAINE

CENTER POINT LARGE PRINT

This Circle Ⓥ Western is published by
Center Point Large Print in 2012 in cooperation with
Golden West Literary Agency.

First Edition, December 2012.

The text of this Large Print edition is unabridged.
In other aspects, this book may
vary from the original edition.
Printed in the United States of America
on permanent paper.
Set in 16-point Times New Roman type.

ISBN: 978-1-61173-588-8

Library of Congress Cataloging-in-Publication Data

Paine, Lauran.
Way of the outlaw : a Western story / Lauran Paine. — 1st ed.
p. cm.
ISBN 978-1-61173-588-8 (lib. bdg. : alk. paper)
1. Large type books. I. Title.
PS3566.A34W39 2012
813'.54—dc23
                                        2012025915

CHAPTER ONE

The heat was a suction that drew moisture from the earth, the air, from living things. It danced and writhed in gelatinous waves. It was almost a physical presence that pressed with lethargic heaviness, and it was accompanied by an evil yellow haze that blurred out the mountains in the background and obscured the prairie.

It was a sullen glitter, a blight upon the land. It pained the eyes, and drove into thin, watery, insufficient shade all living things. Nothing moved around the town or out upon that vast plain. It was midday.

People said of northern New Mexico Territory that it was a sullen and hostile place full of tarantulas, rattlesnakes, Gila monsters, and cruel people. They also said that in its breath-gone summer evenings a man could stretch forth his hand and touch the moon, the red-gold stars. It depended upon the individual's reaction to this raw land, to its endless and ageless silence. Some felt crushed by its hugeness and some responded to its unaltered freshness.

And some, like Troy Warfield, accepted its heat, its changing moods, its immensity, with a philosophical indifference, because they had grown to adulthood in it, or in land just like it.

Warfield appeared upon one of those shimmering northern foothills with the faded sky behind him, with the steady run of plain in front of him, considering that town down there the way one strange dog surveys another strange dog.

He was the only moving thing and for a long while he sat up there just looking. Taking in the sights, the distances, the landmarks, carefully noting everything about this country that lay south of Colorado on his route down into old Mexico.

He was a deliberate man with an iron jaw, wide-spaced eyes that seemed never to be wholly still, and the rawhide-flat and angular build of a life-long rider. He was right at six feet tall, neither an inch under nor an inch over. Right now his steely gaze was hooded behind the half droop of lids, while his wide lips lay closed without pressure for as long as it took him to take the measure of the town down below. He took that measure, much as a fighter measures an opponent, before nudging his leggy bay horse downward from the foothills.

From a mile out that town didn't do much for Troy Warfield. For one thing it was a typical borderland village with its false-fronted wooden buildings, its older, more enduring adobe structures, its dust and its inevitable setting astraddle a stage road from far downcountry to far upcountry. For another thing, since environment molds people, this would be simply another of those semi-desert towns in the New Mexico cow country. The saloons would have different names, the people would have different faces, but the gossip would be just as fallacious and cruel, the interests would be identical, and the reserved acceptance of a stranger wouldn't be any different from the same attitude Warfield had encountered in a dozen similar villages since he'd started traveling southward.

Still, a man on the move had certain basic requirements that only a town could accommodate, so Warfield passed down to the evil yellow-hazed plain and slouched along on his way to that town. Horseshoes wore out, a man's supply of tobacco dwindled, and the need for replenishment of his meager food stocks existed.

Where Warfield came across the stage road, a sign said that town's name was Lincoln. It also gave the population as being two hundred and fifty. It didn't give the name of the county Lincoln was situated in, not that this troubled Warfield, but neither did it give the information that he was seeking—How far was the Mexican border from Lincoln?—and that *did* trouble him.

He passed into Lincoln, and felt the first shade he'd encountered in the little dusty cañon created by opposing sets of store fronts. It was still early afternoon, and the shade was pale and practically useless, but it was shade.

He headed straight for the livery barn, dismounted there, began offsaddling, and by the time he was finished, a copiously sweating older man, wearing a derby hat atop a fine head of skin, came over and studied Warfield, his outfit, and his leggy, big breedy bay horse.

"Fine animal," this liveryman said mechanically.

Warfield finished, turned, and looked at the man. "Take him to the smithy," he said. "Get him shod all around."

The derby hat bobbed up and down.

"Then fetch him back here to your barn, put him in a box stall, grain him light. and hay him heavy."

The derby bobbed again. "Be a dollar six-bits for the shoein' and another dollar for the rest."

Warfield handed across several large silver coins. "Have your day man rub him down good, too. He's earned it, and like you said, mister, he's a fine animal."

Derby Hat accepted the coins, looked at the patiently standing horse, and said: "Built for speed and endurance, that one."

Warfield turned, ran a long glance up and down the opposite store fronts, then looked back. "How much farther to the Mex border?" he asked.

Derby Hat answered at once as though, even while he was studying Warfield's horse, he had been thinking of this distance, too. "Few hundred miles due south." Derby Hat took the bay's lead shank, turned, and went shuffling southward toward the adjoining building, which was Lincoln's blacksmith shop. At the doorway he turned, looked past the bay where Warfield's long, gun-weighted form was passing across toward the place sporting an immense and weathered old rack of elk antlers above the door, and which was appropriately named the Antlers Saloon. Derby Hat remained out there in that wilting sunlight until Warfield disappeared through a pair of louvered doors across the way, then he sucked back a shallow, long breath, and pushed it out again in a sigh, faced forward, and shuffled on inside the sooty blacksmith shop where a short but incredibly massive, broad, and deep-chested man was greedily sucking water out of a soiled old dented dipper.

"George," said Derby Hat, "here's a chore for you. All four feet and all new shoes."

George put down his dipper, swung the back of a filthy hand across his lips to swipe away the residue of that long drink, and turned for a good look at the bay horse. "Well, well," he boomed quietly. "For a change this one's owner ain't a skinflint. New shoes instead of resets." George lifted his sweaty, seamed, and coarse-featured face with its bold and candid little blue eyes, and he smiled. He was a battered man with scars upon him from innumerable brawls with recalcitrant horses, mules, and oxen, not to mention his share of brawling men.

"Fine animal," he said. "Who's he belong to?"

Derby Hat shrugged, his expression turning resignedly caustic. "Stranger passin' through. Tallish younger feller . . . maybe twenty-eight, thirty. Over at the Antlers right now. First question he asked was . . . how far was it to Mexico?" Derby Hat shrugged again.

George walked over, picked up a front hoof, swung around, and took the hoof between his upper legs as he said: "One of *them,* eh? Well, like I've said before, the Lord didn't put me here on this earth to judge folks . . . just to shoe their horses and be amused by 'em."

Derby Hat dropped the lead shank. He seemed loath to step back out into the furious sunlight. He shuffled around the bay where he could watch George work.

"I still say we could be losin' a fortune here in Lincoln by not makin' some effort to check up on these fellers. You know blamed well that of the maybe seventy-five or a hundred who pass through askin' that same question every year, maybe at least fifty of 'em got prices on their heads."

George was levering off the old, thin-worn shoe and didn't look up. But he said, shaking his head to fling off sweat: "What good's money if you're not around to spend it?"

"You always say that," grumbled Derby Hat. "You know blamed well the fellers head for the saloon and drape their dried-out carcasses over the

10

bar . . . with their backs to the door. Hell's bells, even without any he'p from the constable, a couple or three of us businessmen could get the drop, march 'em over to the *calabozo*, lock 'em up, and write for the reward. George, I'm tellin' you within one year we'd be rich."

George put aside his pulling tongs, picked up his farrier's knife, and began to gouge out on either side of the frog. "Dead," he said. "Not rich . . . dead."

"Pshaw!"

George cocked his head upward. Two rivulets of sweat cut through the oily dust on his face but the expression there was unmistakable. George had evidently heard this argument so many times in the past that it annoyed him. He said, those little blue eyes hardening: "You know what I think? I think it's a pretty damned fine line a man draws between what's decent and what's indecent, when he starts bein' greedy. Maybe this one *is* runnin' . . . maybe he done somethin' up north the law wants him for. But goin' to bed at night with a clear conscience is *his* worry . . . not mine. and maybe collectin' three, four hundred dollars . . . which I'd only spend, anyway . . . wouldn't make me a whole lot better'n he is, because sneakin' up behind a feller and gettin' the drop on him for that money would bother my conscience, too."

George waited briefly for comment, but Derby

11

Hat just stood there, quietly sweating, so George went back to work paring at that hoof, only now his powerful arms and shoulders rippled with increased force because he was thinking hard thoughts.

Derby Hat put a hand upon the bellows handle, gave it a downward push, forcing air up under the forge where cherry-red coals glowed, and said: "You're not lookin' at it right. These fellers are criminals . . . wanted men. They broke the law . . . probably murdered folks or robbed banks or rustled livestock. While the rest of us sweat for a livin', they make a lot of money with guns. It's our bound *duty* to help apprehend 'em."

George finished preparing the forehoof for the new shoe, dropped it, straightened up slowly with a grimace from the pain in his back, tossed aside his tools, and went to a rack where he selected a blanked steel shoe. He squinted at this shoe appraisingly, then tossed it into the fire, hit the bellows handle twice to bring on a white-hot heat, and, while waiting, he said to Derby Hat: "We got a constable in Lincoln. It's *his* bound duty to apprehend outlaws. When you or me or some other feller starts gettin' the kind of ideas you're talkin' about it's not because he cares a damned bit about the law, and you know it. It's because he wants some easy money, too . . . the same as that outlaw did . . . and that don't make him a danged bit better'n the outlaw. And I'm goin' to tell you once more . . . you keep flirtin' with this and you're goin' to get killed."

Derby Hat threw up his hands. He half turned as though to march out of the shop, and he froze. Leaning over there just inside the sooty entrance was that lanky man who owned the leggy bay horse. He'd obviously been leaning there, listening to this conversation for some time. Derby Hat's face turned slack and gray while his Adam's apple bobbed up and down, just once, as he swallowed.

Warfield kept gazing over at Derby Hat.

At the forge, George hadn't seen Warfield yet. As he poked the calk end of that reddening shoe deeper into his forge fire, he said to Derby Hat: "Maybe you'd get three, four of these fellers, but directly the word would get around, and one day some fellers'd ride into your barn, get down, ask you your name . . . then shoot you. Just like that. It's happened before. You can't start livin' by the gun and not expect. . . ." George looked up and also saw Warfield standing over there half in sooty gloom, half in reflected light from the roadway. He didn't have to be told who that lanky stranger was. Derby Hat's expression made that painfully obvious.

Warfield straightened up, stepped over, walked around the bay, and afterward halted behind George at the forge. He smiled. It was a slow, wintry kind of a smile.

"I can see you growing old with grandchildren around your knee," Warfield said. "The way a man should grow old." He put his gaze over upon Derby Hat. "I got doubts about you though, mister. Your friend made a good point a while back . . . greed gets folks killed. Inside the law or outside it. Unless you change, you're not going to last long."

Warfield stepped back so the blacksmith could work. He eased down upon a keg half full of horseshoe blanks, crossed one leg over the other, and nodded at George. "I'll just sit here and wait," he said. "Then I'll be on my way."

CHAPTER TWO

It was near evening with a long red gash across the underbelly of heaven when a graying man atop a steeldust gelding came down through Lincoln's roadway dust, turned in at the livery barn, and stepped down. This man, too, was a stranger in town. He stood there holding his reins, gazing down the roadway with a thoughtful, almost cynical, expression. And when Derby Hat came out to take the steeldust, this one said: "Where's a good place to eat?"

Derby Hat pointed on across the road without saying a word. In fact, although he was asked several other questions, he never once unlocked his lips. He'd nod or he'd point, or he'd shake his head, but he would not be drawn into a conversation, and that graying, stockily built, travel-stained stranger looked wonderingly at him, before he walked away, heading for the café.

Lincoln was beginning to come to life now. Riders loped in from the backcountry, townsmen, finished with their days' labors, sought relaxation at the card tables and bars. It was a different town from what it had been much earlier when that first stranger had ridden in, gotten his horse reshod, and had ridden out again. It was cooler, too, not only in town but out upon the range.

That graying man sat at the counter and thoughtfully ate his supper. Beside him, freshly scrubbed but still smelling of horse, black iron, and forge smoke, was the squat, mighty man from the smithy across the road. As he reached over in front of the graying man for one of the forks stuck tines-up in a water glass, he mumbled an apology for reaching.

The graying man nodded and said: "Almost too hot to eat."

The blacksmith considered this a moment, then made a little wry smile. "One of them situations where you're damned if you do and damned if you don't," he said.

The graying man also smiled a little. He was finished now, all but his coffee that he held up in both hands. "Funny thing about the heat," he murmured casually. "I got a habit of carrying peppermint with me when I make one of these midsummer rides. It makes me feel downright cool, and yet, by golly, it's all in my head. I sweat just as much and suffer just as much, actually, only sucking on that peppermint makes me think otherwise."

The blacksmith listened to this and chuckled. "A man's got to outwit himself sometimes," he said. "Today I was shoein' a long-legged bay

16

horse for a feller . . . new shoes all around . . . and I'd taken a drink of water just before I went to work. The more I sweated, the more I had to drink."

"Yeah. I know how that is."

"Well, sort of like your peppermint, I went over, upended the bucket over my shoulders, went back, and worked right on through until I was finished, and, as long as that water . . . and my sweat . . . were dryin' on me, I wasn't thirsty."

The graying man gently nodded, sipped his coffee, and swung to put a studious gaze upon George the blacksmith. "It's the impressions things make," he murmured. "Now, a few minutes ago I rode in over at the livery barn. There was a sort of flabby feller over there wearing a derby hat. He didn't say a word. I asked where I could eat and he pointed over here. I asked him where the rooming house was, and he pointed again. I know blamed well he wasn't a mute and I also know I didn't say anything to make him sulk at me. But my impression was that he was either without the means for talking or was upset about something and couldn't shake it off long enough to be civil."

George brought up some coins, counted them meticulously, and placed several of them upon the counter beside his emptied plate. He screwed up his forehead, looked around at the graying stranger as a man might look who'd discovered that what had started out as a light, very casual exchange between strangers, had suddenly become not so light and casual.

"That feller you're talkin' about got quite a shock this afternoon," he said, stood up, nodded, and walked on out of the café.

There were other men in the café. It appeared to be a place where the single merchants of Lincoln congregated at mealtimes. There were also several cowboys. The graying man sipped and gazed quietly around. His eyes never obtrusively lingered but neither did they skip over a single face; he seemed to have that developed sense of observation some men had that enabled him to see things closely without seeming to.

He was about average height, perhaps even an inch or two below average height. His age could have been anywhere from thirty to forty-four or forty-five, for, although his hair was gray at the temples, giving him an unmistakable appearance of seasoned good age, his face had scarcely a line on it, except around the eyes; there, the lines were small, criss-crossing crow's-feet. They had come there not altogether from habitual squinting in a raw, sun-blasted land. They were the lines caused by shrewd calculation, shrewd observation, and thoughtfulness.

This was U.S. Marshal John Trent, a man whose almost nondescript, very average appearance had enabled him to build a reputation around his name that was almost a legend, because until he introduced himself, which Trent did not often do, people had visions of this notorious lawman as being nearly ten feet tall, as implacable as death itself, and as deadly as a whole troop of cavalry.

He finished his coffee, tossed down payment, and walked out into the fading evening. There was a rising breath of air coming fragrantly from the punished roadway; here and there wooden store fronts popped as the wood cooled after daytime's furious heat.

There was a solemn blandness to this night, a kind of melancholy resignation that accompanied the faint scent of greasewood, sage, cured grass. This was the half-light, half-dark hour of total loneliness for strangers, when being far from home brought up in them all the quiet memories.

Trent made a cigarette out front of the café, lit it, and saw that powerful blacksmith walking along toward the northward saloon with elk antlers bolted overhead. He watched and he speculated. Trent was a man who knew men. That blacksmith had been some part of whatever had happened here today involving the liveryman. It was one of the idiosyncrasies of this sparse, hard life that men were wise in the ways of keeping their own counsel where the law and what it stood for was not always available to give protection.

Trent smoked on. He was tired and he was

dehydrated. He knew where Lincoln's rooming house was—a bed with a genuine set of springs under it could seem more desirable than a handsome woman to a man in his condition. But Trent had a feeling. It wasn't anything he could pin down or even define, yet it was a solid premonition in the dark places of his mind. He'd felt it before, near the end of a trail.

He dropped the smoke, stepped on it, turned, and walked north toward that same saloon the blacksmith had entered. As a hound dog picks up his wanted scent, so did John Trent obey the proddings of that feeling he had.

The Antlers Saloon was one out of many just like it. There was one large, barn-like room with an iron stove in a far corner, with tables and chairs scattered back along the walls, and with a worn-smooth old bar running along the far wall with shelves and pictures behind it. There were also the typical patrons—cowboys, merchants from the town itself, freighters, stage men, a few traveling men, here and there old-timers whose world, once large and violent and colorful, was now shrunk to the size of these four rough walls where they idled away their sundown years in a good, masculine atmosphere, picking up a free drink now and then, and living for little else.

Generally the customers knew one another. There was a little joking back and forth, a little careless comradeship, and occasionally the quick flash of a spun coin to see which of two men would stand the drinks.

Trent blended into this tobacco-hazed atmosphere as easily as a lizard on a rock. His expression was easy, near to smiling, his dusty attire and tied-down .45 were nondescript. Only Trent's eyes held a veiled but sharper look until he spotted the blacksmith, then they became as good naturedly indifferent as all the other eyes in that restless room.

He eased in beside George and called for a beer. He stood there, one spurred boot draped across the brass rail underfoot, quietly sipping.

George was having a straight shot of rye whiskey. He turned, recognized the graying man, nodded, and got a carefully smoothed-out expression upon his scarred countenance.

Trent understood. He put down the beer glass, half twisted from the middle, and said: "You know what we could do, friend? We could play this game for half the night, me askin', you duckin' around the questions." Trent beckoned to the barman, pointed to their glasses, and said to George: "But you put in a hard day. So did I." He leaned over the bar, waited out the barman, then lifted his replenished glass and gazed into its bubbly amberness. "Which way did he ride out?"

George hadn't touched his whiskey glass. He swung his head though, and he said: "Who?"

"The feller who had his horse fresh shod with new shoes all around, friend."

"All I told you. . . ."

"Was that you'd shod a feller's leggy bay horse all around, friend," interrupted Trent. He sipped, looked through the upheld glass again, and said: "I could describe those shoes to you . . . the ones you pulled off. One had the outside calk worn smooth, another was split at the toe. Friend, I've been trailing the horse that wore those shoes too long, too far. I've had a hard day, too."

"How do you know it's the same man, mister?"

Trent put the glass down and looked squarely at George. "How many leggy bay horses have you shod today that were being ridden by strangers?"

George didn't answer. He took up his shot glass, balanced it, tipped his head, and downed the fiery liquor. After that he rapidly blinked for a moment before he said: "South. He rode south."

"What happened with the liveryman, friend?"

George blew out raw breath. That whiskey had been very green. "He was talkin' about gettin' the drop on some of these drifters that come down here on their way over the line into Mexico. He's talked like that before . . . only this time that feller who owned the leggy bay horse had walked up without either of us hearin' him, and was standin' in the shadows of my shop, listenin'."

Trent smiled. His eyes came to a gradual twinkle. He suddenly laughed. He could imagine it all now, and it struck him funny, particularly since he'd seen that derby-hatted liveryman who was anything but a brave man.

The blacksmith didn't laugh; he didn't even smile. But he looked understandingly at Trent. "That feller figured on stayin' in town until that happened. After that, he sat there until I finished, paid me, went back after his saddle, and rode on out . . . southward."

Trent shook his head at the barman's inquiring look. He faced George again with the hum of voices all around them, with the tobacco smoke growing steadily thicker as the evening turned to solid night outside. "Your friend," he said evenly, "is a fool. One of these days he'll get killed." Then Trent walked on out of the saloon.

There was a rash of opaque stars overhead now, and a lop-sided old moon was serenely floating across the great vault of heaven. A scratch of light blazed briefly across infinity where a falling star turned to cinder and rained earthward in fragments.

Trent looked over where the rooming house stood. He also considered the livery barn where a pair of lamps burned inside, hanging from rafters to light the runway. Warfield hadn't eaten or rested. Neither had his horse. Neither had Trent rested—but he'd eaten and his horse had both

23

eaten and rested. It wasn't much of an edge, but sometimes this was all it took.

If you pushed them hard enough, sooner or later you gained an infinitesimal advantage. The trick of pursuit was to know when you had that much of an edge, and how to exploit it.

Trent knew. The horse was the critical thing. A man could suffer a little. He could catnap in the saddle or he could take his belt up an extra notch. But he had to have a strong animal under him.

Well, here in this god-forsaken little cow town it had finally happened. After seven hundred miles—and with about three hundred left to go—Trent had finally gotten an edge. That's all he'd been waiting for, just enough of an advantage to enable him to overtake Warfield.

"Mister . . . ?"

Trent turned. The thickly made blacksmith was standing there.

"You're the law, aren't you?"

Trent nodded. "Yeah, friend, I'm the law."

"What did he do that you're after him so hard?"

"He murdered," said Trent softly, and kept staring at the blacksmith until George turned, stepped down into the roadway, set his shoulders, and walked straight on over toward the livery barn.

Trent somberly watched the blacksmith disappear over where those interior hanging lanterns were. He waited a little longer, then he, too, crossed the roadway.

Now, there was music coming from the saloons; there were off-key masculine voices being raised in discordant singing. Sometimes it didn't take much to give release to bone-dry gullets and repressed spirits in hot summertime. Sometimes only a couple of beers did it.

Trent walked into the livery barn, saw the blacksmith and liveryman in earnest conversation farther along, and bellowed for his horse. The liveryman started in his boots. He hastened after Trent's animal, and the blacksmith glanced up, saw Trent, turned, and walked on out through the rear of the barn.

Trent turned to view the little town. A half hour from now Lincoln would be another shadowy place in his memory. He sighed, thinking of that bed with springs under it. When his horse came along, saddled and bridled, Trent scarcely wasted a glance at the liveryman except to say: "What's the next town, friend, and how far from here is it?"

"Fourteen miles, and it's called Daggett."

Trent flipped the liveryman $1 from atop the saddle, reined around, and went riding stolidly southward on out of Lincoln with the night closing instantly around him. He still had an edge.

CHAPTER THREE

Lying back, his body all loose and easy, Warfield listened to the pleasant night, listened to his horse's shifting, freshly shod hoofs on the hard ground as the hungry animal nibbled on graze and the none-too-nourishing cured grass. Total relaxation came to Warfield and the surrounding scents and sounds comforted him in his complete loneliness. They were familiar. They were old and pleasant, and a part of his life clear back to its earliest years.

There was simplicity to the sound of a horse moving, of its strong teeth grinding over fodder. There was an age-old reality to the smell of summertime dust in cool night air. And there was something in the timeless heavens turning purple that reached for a man's spirit, cradled it in a gentle grip of endlessness, which was both promise and surcease.

A man was put upon this earth to be a part of dust and loneliness, to be a part of struggle and suffering. To feel with every pore of his hide the hardness of life, and to take his small pleasures during the intervening periods of relaxation—like now, lying there ten white-hot miles south of a place called Lincoln, on the way to another town the name of which he didn't even know. Lying there under that scatter of pale stars, under that old pewter moon, surrounded by the formless night, safe and at peace.

Warfield had a smoke between his fingers. Its tangy fragrance was good. Tobacco was always good to a man who'd run out days before. It was one of those little pleasures, like a drink of cold water after a hard ten hours in the saddle on a hot day that a man relished.

But a lonely man has lonely thoughts, try as he may to close them out, so Warfield sat up finally, inhaled, exhaled, stubbed out his smoke, and put his head in his hands remembering the secret things in a woman's glance, remembering her long silence as she gazed at him, remembering the tilt of her head in star shine and the solemn knowledge she'd shown him that last time. A solid knowledge that told him in complete silence that she knew what life was, not what it ought to be.

Something came over that bridgeless distance separating them to touch Warfield briefly, to bring a quick, squeezing pain to his heart, so he got up, dusted off, and walked over to watch the horse graze.

New shoes were fine. The bay wouldn't go lame now. But new shoes were no substitute for an empty gut, and no matter how much of this roughage the bay ate, he'd still be tucked up in the flank and heavy on the bit when they resumed their way.

Warfield thought of Derby Hat back in that last town and his long mouth drooped unpleasantly at that recollection. Except for Derby Hat, Warfield would have spent the night back there, the bay would have gotten a decent bit of fodder, and by dawn they'd have both been on the trail again, refreshed and ready.

Down the southward night, on across the ghostly plain, lay a cluster of town lights. On a clear summertime night a man could see twenty miles. But those lights weren't more than four, five miles away. Warfield, thinking of a bed with springs under it, pondered the wisdom of pushing along. But he didn't ponder very long; a man's horse was his life insurance. He had to take particular care of his bay. Another time, years back, he might have struck out for that town, but not now. The horse was all-important now. Somewhere back there was a man with graying temples astride a durable steeldust gelding with a U.S. marshal's German-silver circlet in his pocket. Warfield had to favor his breedy bay or the steeldust would win, and he couldn't permit that to happen. Life was good. Maybe at times it was hard and cruel, but a man never hated it, never considered voluntarily surrendering it.

Warfield went back where his saddle lay,

dropped down, and closed his eyes. Sleep came quickly, as a sort of blessing, relieving Warfield of any further need for resistance to his secret thoughts. He was dog-tired and although he'd picked up a few tins of food back at Lincoln, he hadn't bought very many of them because they constituted a dead weight, so he'd eaten, but very sparingly, and had gone to sleep on a shrunken gut that nagged a little. He felt vaguely and uneasily that somehow that town back there had been some kind of a crucial turning in his life, but he hadn't been able to see exactly how this might be, except that his horse had been denied needed rest and food, so he'd gone to sleep with only the very faintest of troubling thoughts.

And he awakened the same way, with the moon far down and the night much cooler, that uneasy feeling still in him. But in the confusion of any troubled man's mind lay all manner of suspicions, all manner of doubts and skepticisms, so Warfield arose concentrating only on hitting the trail without a lot of thinking that would lead him nowhere.

He rigged out his bay horse, rose up to settle over leather, and reined out, always southward. Within slightly less than an hour he was parallel with that town but off to the west so that its pre-dawn shape and silence lay on his left. There had been only one thing he'd wanted from that town— a decent place to rest—and, since he was now rested, he rode on past with pre-dawn's silent grayness shielding him from view, if anyone over there had been looking, which they weren't.

The southward land heaved away mile upon mile of it, seemingly endless, with always some peaks and hills standing east and west under the strengthening light of new day. He crossed a gravelly dry creekbed, skirted a land swell that curved inward slightly from south to west, passed a bosque of cottonwoods, the first he'd seen in many days, sighted a ranch dead ahead, and angled out and around it with his careful attention never resting for fear some inadvertent meeting with cowboys might come about. But it didn't, and he left the ranch behind and for many miles afterward there was nothing.

The sun steadily climbed, turning his world a faded, brassy hue. The heat piled up, brought dark sweat out to make Warfield's shirt cling to him, and robbed Warfield's bay of his energy.

That browse the big leggy animal had filled up on the night before was excellent roughage, but it did not reinvigorate the horse at all, so now he plodded along mechanically, head hung and lethargic, which troubled Warfield. He could not afford to have his horse play out on him, not out here, not this close to security. He would have to go into a town, and soon, otherwise the bay's reserves of strength would be too depleted and no matter how much rest and grain he got, there would be for him no quick recovery. If that happened, Warfield was finished.

He could buy another horse. Even rope one out of some corral or pasture in the night. But two things discouraged him in this. One was very elemental, too. If he abandoned the bay, Trent would inevitably find it and know how close he was to Warfield. The other was that this particular horse was a thoroughbred; he had never in his life been outrun, and it was this particular ability that Warfield was now relying most heavily upon. In the final showdown, that incredible speed could very easily make the difference between life and death for Troy Warfield. No horse he could buy in this southern country would have that same high-bred attribute.

Miles south of the town Warfield had by-passed, and, with the punishing sun cruelly bearing down, a deer sprang up from its bed beside a mesquite clump and rattled down into an arroyo, leaving behind the scent of alkali dust and musk. Warfield scarcely heeded. He was riding now with that strength-conserving looseness that experienced range men employed on endless rides, his hat tipped forward to shield eyes that dryly grated in their sockets, his body swinging in relaxed cadence to the steps of his mount, the drying perspiration giving him a mote of relief.

It was late afternoon before he halted, a time when the sun reddened, the sky turned steely, and the fiercest heat should have begun diminishing. But it didn't because Warfield was now upon the edge of the desert. He stopped at a large old stone watering trough, got down, and pushed his hatless head all the way to the shoulders into the tepid water, while beside him his horse drank and sweated and drank some more.

Afterward, being cooled by that water, he made a smoke and lit it, turned slowly and gazed out and around, saw the saddled horse standing, hip-shot, under a low-limbed ancient juniper, and gradually drew up to an alert stiffness seeking the person who was also out here somewhere.

He didn't find that person, not at once anyway, and eventually it was the other person who found Warfield. He was a boy of fourteen or fifteen, tall and straight as an arrow with a tumbling shock of unruly fair hair. He walked forward from up out of a distant arroyo with something in his arms. He'd seen Warfield. There was no hint of suspicion, of doubt in the lad's tilted, sun-bronzed face as he walked on up. He seemed in need of something he could not himself provide, knew it, and therefore came with beseeching eyes up to the stone trough.

He had a half-grown mongrel pup in his arms. The dog was limp and dirty and covered with what appeared to be the saliva, mixed with blood, of a larger animal.

"What happened?" Warfield asked, looking

long and carefully over toward that arroyo the lad had come up out of.

"Big ol' grayback coyote tied into him. I tried to call him back but he's just a pup, mister. The coyote went down into that arroyo, the pup jumped down after him, and before I could get over there, I heard him screamin'."

Warfield dropped his eyes to the pup. "They'll do that," he observed. "You live hereabouts?"

"Two miles west. We ranch over there. Mister, can you do anything for him?"

"You alone out here, son?"

"Just me 'n' the pup. We were rabbit huntin'. Can you help him, mister?"

Warfield bent slightly from the waist. The little dog was breathing but his eyes were cold and his nose was dry. He took him gently in both hands, turned, and immersed him up to his snout in the trough, then he went to work seeking the location of the coyote bites. As he did this, he eased down upon the trough's stone edge and talked.

"When I was your age, I knew better'n to do what you did, son. There's hardly a dog living that can whip a coyote, but a pup this size . . . he never had a chance."

"He ran off though, mister. He acted scairt."

"Naw," said Warfield scornfully. "I'm surprised a feller like you doesn't know more about coyotes. They're smart. Smarter than foxes and sometimes smarter than men. He wasn't running away . . . he was simply leading your pup, staying just far enough ahead to lure him on. Then he ducked down into that arroyo, cut back, and got set. When your pup jumped down there . . . crunch!"

The boy's anguished eyes were brimful of unshed tears. "How bad off is he . . . will he die, mister?"

Warfield didn't answer that for a long time. Not until he'd completed his minute examination. Then he shook his head. "He'll live. But you've got to get him home. Fix up a box in the barn, somewhere it's cool and sort of dark. Dogs need cool darkness when they don't feel good. Feed him plenty of porridge and milk and don't let the blowflies get to him." Warfield threw an almost unconscious look out over the shimmering countryside. "Your pa's probably got some blue-vitriol ointment around. Put it on the wounds. Keep him quiet . . . and, boy, after this don't take a pup like this hunting with you without having a gun along, too."

The boy listened carefully, and, as Warfield passed him back his limp little furry bundle, he said: "Mister, why don't you come along home with me?"

It was a spontaneously asked question, the kind a boy would ask a man when he had no reservations in his mind about the man. Warfield sat there on the old stone trough, gazing at the lad. Two miles west and in this empty world he could possibly find exactly what he needed—rest and provender for the bay. He idly kicked one leg back and forth.

"Your pa run cattle?" he asked.

"Yes, but he pulled out early this mornin' bound for Daggett to fetch back supplies and rock salt for the animals. He'll be home tomorrow sometime."

"Just you and your ma at home now?"

"No, my sister's there, too. But Paw sent her to the upper place to check some heifers up there that're springing."

"You got close neighbors, son?"

The boy shook his head, shifted his hold on the little dog, and waited.

Warfield smiled. "My name's Troy," he said. "What's yours?"

"Will Crockett, same as my paw."

Warfield stood up. "Lead out, Will," he said. "My horse could use some hay and grain, and I could use some rest."

They departed from the spring area, riding due west with dying day all around them, with shadows beginning to form thinly and with the smoke haze softening. But there still was no lessening of that punishing heat.

Young Will rode ahead, leading the way, and although he turned to look back every once in a while, he didn't speak to Warfield unless Warfield spoke to him.

The pup whimpered shortly before they came within sight of the buildings ahead. "He hurts," said the boy, sounding distressed.

Warfield was assessing those buildings as he answered. "Yeah, he hurts. And he'll hurt a lot more tomorrow, too. But maybe he'll learn. There are some things in this life it just doesn't pay to tangle with."

The boy nodded. He had his reins looped, his horse walking quietly along homeward bound with a horse's solid instinctiveness. "One time my paw told me somethin' about like that, Mister Troy. He said there are some things that even when a man beats 'em, he doesn't really come out on top because they never forget and they always come back to try a feller again and again."

Warfield looked queerly at the boy, rode along almost as far as the ranch yard, then he said: "Tell me, Will, how come your pa to settle 'way down here?"

Will shrugged, looked around the yard ahead as though seeking someone, and indifferently said: "I guess because he liked it."

CHAPTER FOUR

When a man knows advantage is coming over to his side, when he can predict tomorrow as easily as he can recall yesterday, he feels within himself a letting down of all sense of urgency. It's almost as though he and destiny are one and the same thing.

That was how Trent felt as he sat in Daggett's most affluent saloon whiling away the night, waiting. He knew, after an hour's careful searching, that Warfield hadn't yet arrived in town. He thought he was still somewhere between Lincoln and Daggett, coming steadily southward as he'd never failed to do thus far. So he sat there at the green-cloth-covered poker table nursing his drink and considering Daggett's town marshal, and feeling certain.

The town marshal was a bear of a slow-moving, dogged man with a craggy face chiseled out of an environment that had seldom been mild. He might lack imagination, but he didn't lack that animal courage that was so essential to survival here in this desert world. His name was Chalmers. He was about forty years of age, and, when he lifted his eyes to view graying John Trent, there was a world of undisguised admiration in his glance.

"Maybe he figured he was far enough ahead to risk a catnap. Maybe he won't show up in Daggett till later, when there ain't so many folks stirring."

Trent was very comfortable in a chair with his legs pushed out to their limit beneath the table, with that liquor lying in his stomach. He said: "It's close to the end now, Marshal. For more than seven hundred miles it's been a race of endurance, but Warfield made his one mistake back at Lincoln . . . he didn't give his horse a chance."

Chalmers turned thoughtful. "If he'd stayed there though, with you closin' the distance like that, you'd have come into Lincoln before he'd have pulled out, so maybe, even though he made his mistake, he's bought himself a little more time."

Trent shrugged. "After seven hundred miles I can write off a town or two. Lincoln or Daggett, it's all the same. He'll be along. He's got to trade a little time for the well-being of that bay thoroughbred. There's nothing else he can do. He's no kid, Marshal . . . he knows what lies ahead over that desert. And I'm here ahead of him."

"You need sleep," observed Chalmers. "Even a man as tough as you are, Mister Trent, needs rest sometime. Even an Apache couldn't keep goin' like this. I know my town, its folks, and every dark corner . . . you go get some rest on one of the cots over at the jailhouse and I'll keep the vigil, Mister Trent."

Around them the saloon's noises came and went. There was the soft fall of chips, the clink of glasses against bottles, the constant run of masculine voices. It was like a familiar pattern to Trent, and it seldom varied. Release from the everyday stress and strain of living seemed always to fall into the identical framework in cattle country.

New Mexico wasn't a whole lot different from Colorado. It was a world of extremes, of searing dryness and unreasoning cloudbursts, of drowsy summertime peacefulness and the wild flash of gunfire. It was a huge territory, raw and primitive. It burned softness out of a man, turned him resourceful, watchful, and oftentimes fierce. It put a look upon a man's bronzed face that never wholly departed even after he migrated to other, softer places. But not many departed because the West was a man's land and even in its cruelest moments he stayed on.

Trent thought on these things as he sat there sipping whiskey, all loose and easy in his chair. He faintly shook his head at Chalmers. "It's my affair," he murmured. "I've pushed too hard and come too far not to be on hand at the finish. Thanks anyway."

Across the room near the bar an angry woman exploded toward a wispy, youthful man with yellow hair and a tied-down, bone-handled .45. She slapped him, making a sound with that blow that carried because the steady hum of voices had atrophied at her first angry words. In a twinkling everyone was watching those two. Marshal Chalmers pushed his chair around, making the only sound as that youngish man brought his face back toward the girl. There was a livid imprint upon his left cheek, otherwise his face was white. Trent saw the little ripple where jaw muscles tightened and a bulge appeared along the young man's jaw. His eyes, which were pale, got suddenly very bright.

Chalmers, heaving up out of his chair, said: "That's enough."

If he'd meant to stalk over there, he didn't get the chance. With a blur and a slight lift of one shoulder, that bone-handled six-gun was out and up and leveled. Chalmers stopped in his tracks, blinking at that gun.

"Mind your own business, you old fool," said the young man softly. "Butt in where you ain't wanted and you'll go out of here feet first."

There wasn't a sound in the place. Trent, with his left hand raised, still sipped whiskey, still sat over there, loose and easy, with his legs run out their full length under the table. He was carefully watching that yellow-haired cowboy. He knew the breed—another tumbleweed from the plains or the mountains or the cruel desert. Another drifter who had caught the scent of perfumed hair, who had been drawn to a woman like steel to a magnet, all his age-old instincts rushing over him, changing him completely from what he otherwise might have been—a good enough hand with a lariat, a branding iron, a spoiled mean horse, or a fry pan at some mescal fire behind the chuck wagon. A man who'd share his last drink of water or hand over his last clean shirt.

And there he stood upon the brink of murder, one breath away from doing something that would forever change him. And for what? Nothing. Within ten days he wouldn't even be able to recall her face.

Trent slowly put down his whiskey glass, slowly said: "Now what, cowboy? Back out the door?" Trent shook his head. "You'd never make it. Put up the gun."

Those narrowed blue eyes drifted a fraction of an inch past Chalmers to Trent. The younger man's whole figure, unmoving as it was, seemed to tighten, to present menace to this new threat. But the eyes showed none of that same rancor, probably because Trent looked so entirely casual and harmless sitting there, his hat pushed far back, his whiskery face showing weariness, his unmoving gaze flat and dull and slightly hooded, not with any direct threat at all, but instead with cool interest.

"A man's hungers can be his worst enemies,"

went on Trent. "You pull that trigger and nothing afterward will ever again be the same for you. Put the thing away, cowboy. Buy a drink and that'll be the end of it."

There wasn't a sound anywhere now, or a movement.

Death in capital letters was standing behind everyone's shoulder, waiting. Trent let the cowboy's flat stare slide by. He picked up his whiskey glass and slowly raised it with his left hand. Over the rim he said: "Believe me when I tell you I know what comes next . . . the running, the hiding, the being caught . . . the hanging, if you're lucky. If not, dragging yourself behind a rock somewhere with your middle on fire from bullets, and leaking out your life in the dust where no one gives a damn."

"For a preacher," said the cowboy softly, flintily, "you sure like your whiskey, stranger."

"I'm not a preacher," replied Trent, still balancing his shot glass. "I'm a federal United States marshal . . . and right this minute I've got a Forty-Five aimed at your belly under this table." Trent paused.

The tension drew out to its absolute limit. The cowboy's pale gaze flickered downward. Then instantly lifted to Trent's face again.

"A man's got his pride, Marshal," murmured the cowboy.

"I wouldn't bruise your pride," said Trent. "I'm

not ordering you to holster that gun. I'm *asking* you to. I'm saying *please*."

"Yeah? Then what, Marshal? Six months in Daggett's lousy jailhouse?"

"Walk on out of here, get on your horse, and cool off under the stars, friend."

"I got your word?"

Trent nodded. He felt Chalmers's indignant stare swing half around and bore into him, but he nodded again anyway. "You got my word, friend."

The cowboy's nostrils quivered. He glanced elsewhere around the room. The woman was still standing there, her face twisted and ugly with fear, but the cowboy didn't even see her. He let off a breath, holstered his weapon, and stood there.

"*Adiós*," said Trent, finishing the last of his whiskey, putting the glass aside, and watching.

The cowboy started toward the door with little stiff steps. As he passed Trent, he said roughly: "I won't forget, Marshal. *Adiós*." He passed on out into the silent night.

Chalmers stood watching Trent. Around the room other men also considered him.

When the abrupt, harsh sound of a hard-hooked horse racing down the night came into that silence, a mustached bartender slapped the bar with his wiping rag and boomed out: "Drinks on the house, boys. Drinks on the house!"

Trent and that barman exchanged a fleeting look. They were worlds apart in everything except

43

the fact that both had gray above the ears, both had lived. And if there was no place in this raw land for compassion, still, men possessed it in their secret hearts, even the toughest of them.

Chalmers sank back down into his vacated chair. He scowled into his empty glass, refilled it, and turned it in its own little sticky pool. He sat there thinking some private thoughts for a while, then he faintly shrugged, leaned over to refill Trent's glass, too, and he raised his left hand.

"You done right. Even lettin' him walk on out. I expect to me and any other average feller, that drawed gun was like wavin' a red cape before a bull. But, Mister Trent, I see now why you're famous as a peace officer. Here's to your health and long life."

They drank. Trent shifted a little on his chair. There was the sound of a gun sliding down across leather on his right side, and he said, without smiling: "Marshal, when you know you're going to kill *one,* it makes you feel different toward the others that aren't set upon the wrong trail yet. I apologize for butting into your business."

Chalmers looked rueful. "He was faster'n lightning. He'd have got me sure. I'm figurin' it's maybe me ought to be doin' the apologizin'."

"Who was he?"

Chalmers wagged his head. "Don't think I ever saw him before. They come and they go. You know how it is."

A tall, dusty man hiked past, nodded at Chalmers, saying: " 'Evenin', Marshal." This stranger put a careful gaze upon Trent, gravely nodded to him, also, and went on up to the bar.

Chalmers said indifferently: "Will Crockett. He's got a place south and west of town. Desert rancher." Then Chalmers pushed back and stood up. "Time to make my rounds, Mister Trent. Care to come along? We can hit the public corral and livery barn . . . just in case Warfield's snuck in without us knowin' it."

Trent got up, hitched at his shell belt, and walked through a sea of veiled, carefully interested glances on out into the yonder night with his companion.

It was late. Daggett's homes and stores were black and shrouded. Along Main Street the saloons and gambling rooms showed light. So did the livery barn, the jailhouse, and the local hotel, but, otherwise, the place was so darkly quiet the footfalls of Trent and Marshal Chalmers sounded unusually loud.

At the livery barn a bearded, big old man shook his head somberly to all Chalmers's questions about a stranger riding in on a leggy bay horse.

"Been no one come in at all since nine o'clock, and even them warn't strangers . . . 'twas local young folks out sparkin' with buggies." The bearded man shook his head at Chalmers, his sunken set eyes glowing with a firm light of powerful disapproval. "I tell you, Marshal, the younger generation's skiddin' straight to hell, and I don't know what ails their parents these days . . . lettin' them go buggy ridin' in the night until nine, ten o'clock. The morals o' the country are deterioratin' fast, and that's a fact."

Chalmers led Trent out of there, stopped upon the plank walk, peered around to make sure that bearded, big old man wasn't listening, and said: "He's the lay preacher for the Methodists around here . . . when there's a congregation to preach to, which isn't too often." Chalmers wryly waggled his head and started off.

Trent went along, near to smiling. Sometimes the bad ones in this life seemed more tolerable than the good ones.

Without encountering either Warfield or his thoroughbred horse, they made a complete circuit of Daggett, even going as far as the shanties a quarter mile from town.

The last half hour of this inspection turned Trent quiet. Somehow, probably by surrendering to weariness long before he sighted Daggett, Warfield had eluded Trent.

Once, he and Chalmers thought they might have stumbled onto him, at least onto something unusual. They heard a man snoring in the back of a battered wagon. But when they got over to investigate, Chalmers drew back with a disappointed grunt, and said: "Will Crockett, that desert cowman who came into the saloon right before we left, sleepin' in the back of his rig. The hell with it, Mister Trent, come on down to the jailhouse and we'll have a pot of coffee."

Trent went but he no longer made good company.

He knew now, with dawn not too far off, that he'd not only lost another night's much needed rest, but that Warfield wasn't going to appear in Daggett after all.

He decided to strike out southward again, right after he'd freshened up on hot coffee. His horse was at the livery barn rested, fed, and rubbed down.

It occurred to him as he stepped into Chalmers's office that his own weariness and the comparable weariness of Warfield's leggy bay thoroughbred lessened Trent's advantage. But he refused to acknowledge that, this close, he should rest.

CHAPTER FIVE

Warfield met Mrs. Crockett, a drab, worked-out woman whose eyes mirrored some vague regret, and, between the three of them, they made Will's pup comfortable in a box in the rickety barn. Will couldn't find the ointment but his mother knew where it was. She kneeled there beside them, watching Warfield's practiced hands move with surprising gentleness, and, afterward, it showed plain in her eyes that she wondered about him.

They had supper at the house with Mrs. Crockett worrying a little about Abbie. "She's had plenty of time to ride out and ride back," she told Warfield over their coffee. " 'Course it's warm, so maybe she waited out the sun."

"Probably," assented Warfield. "If you'd like, Will and I could go look for her."

"No," said Mrs. Crockett quickly. "No, Mister Troy, you look weary. She'll be along. It's only that a mother worries."

Warfield stood up. He washed up outside at the well box and it made a difference. He still needed a shave, but in the poor light of one coal-oil lamp in that dingy kitchen he looked more worn-down than soiled or unkempt. "I'm mighty obliged for the supper," he said, moving gracefully toward the door.

Will jumped up to go out into the night with him.

Mrs. Crockett looked him squarely in the eyes, and smiled. "It wasn't much, but you were certainly welcome to it, Mister Troy." She kept gazing straight at him and he saw in her what he'd overlooked before—a strong and fatalistic acceptance of things, of everything she had seen and lived through, an indomitable reliance. Whatever lay locked in her secret heart, whatever wistfulness had put that underlying other faint expression upon her face, she would not complain because she was inherently stronger than anything that had happened to her, or than anything she wistfully dreamed of. She would never abandon her dreams, but neither would they ever derange her.

He inclined his head slightly, coming in that silent moment of exchanged glances to respect Will Crockett's mother, then he walked on out of the house with Will at his heels, paced along to the barn where his breedy horse was steadily eating, first grain then meadow hay, and kneeled beside the pup's box. The little battered animal looked up and weakly thumped his tail.

The boy dropped down at once with a murmur of relief and strong affection.

Warfield stood watching briefly, then went over to watch his horse eat. He was bone-tired but the sound of those powerful jaws working, and the look of his horse filling out in that cribbed old stall made the load upon Warfield's spirit lift a little.

The night was advancing and at long last there was a breath of coolness to it. It worked its lulling effect upon Warfield so well that at first he didn't hear the steady, unhurrying approach of that ridden horse. But young Will did, and he jumped up to run to the doorway and look out.

"Abbie?"

A girl's fluting call came back instantly. "It's all right, Will! I just waited for sundown."

She rode on up and stepped down. From back in the gloomy barn Warfield stood like stone. He could see her out there, could definitely distinguish by profile that she wasn't anyone to fear, but all the same it took a moment for the pounding of his heart to cease.

Will was talking to her, his words rushing together with excitement. He explained what had happened to his pup, how he'd found Warfield, and how Warfield had come home with him. He was still talking fast as the long-legged, high-breasted girl packed her saddle inside, saw Warfield standing there, and became perfectly still. She'd obviously only been half listening.

Warfield stepped up, relieved her of the saddle,

turned, and hung it from a post peg by one stirrup, turned back with a slow smile meant to be reassuring, took the bridle and blanket, hung them up, also, and faced forward as young Will stammered out a clumsy formal introduction.

Abbie wasn't at all the little sister Warfield had carelessly imagined. She was at least eighteen, perhaps nineteen years old. Her hair was light, like Will's, and curly. It clung to her head. Her face was pretty with large, steady gray eyes—like her mother's eyes—and a heavy, wide mouth that had a slight lilting lift at the outer corners. Something passed out of her over to Warfield making him acutely conscious of her as a woman.

Will was calling now, wanting her to see the miraculous recovery his pup was making. She broke off staring at Warfield, finally, and walked on over. But even as she stood there, lean and long and clean-limbed in the dingy barn gloom, Warfield could tell from her disturbed expression that she was still thinking of him. Slowly he paced his way on out into the bland night, leaned upon the yonder hitch rack, and went to work manufacturing a smoke.

There was a time in every man's life when the decent good things he'd been taught from the cradle seemed regrettable, seemed pointlessly senseless and trying. Abbie was as lovely a girl as Warfield had seen in a long time. He lit up, exhaled, turned his back upon the barn, and watched the night firm up in its purple glory. She walked past behind him, bound for the house. He didn't look around, not at first anyway. Not until she was half across the dusty yard, then he did.

But a man with a memory in his heart lived a life that was not his own. Abbie appeared as a breath of hope in an otherwise dreary race for survival, but even that quick, hard shock he'd initially gotten at sight of her didn't drown that other feeling, so Warfield stood there smoking, watching the night firmly settle, and didn't move again until Will came over and leaned there beside him.

He looked up at Warfield with soft, admiring eyes. "You sure know what to do," he said softly.

Warfield looked down and around with smoke trickling past his nostrils. "Your pa would have known, Will. When a man spends his best years in the service of things of the soil . . . he gets a sort of wisdom."

"My paw doesn't like dogs," said Will. "He didn't like it when I found this one and fetched him home. He says they bark too much, chase chickens, and eat too much."

Warfield killed his smoke and kept looking at the boy. Sometimes a man could get a clear picture of another man without ever meeting him. Sometimes just a look or a careless word was enough.

"Well, sometimes dogs *do* bark too much," said

Warfield, stepping gingerly here. "When I was a kid, you know how folks broke pups of killing chickens?"

"No. How?"

"Well, they'd take the dead chicken and tie it around the pup's neck and make him wear it until it got pretty ripe. Folks said the smell of that chicken'd make a dog so darned sick of chickens he'd ever afterward leave 'em alone."

"Does it work, Mister Troy? We don't have many chickens but maybe someday my dog'll kill one so I ought to know how to break him."

Warfield didn't know whether it worked or not. He couldn't remember, so he said: "If your pup ever kills a chicken, you try it. I reckon though, that what'd work for one pup might not work for another. The same as with men." Then Warfield smiled and his strong white teeth shone in the night. "I'll bet you one thing though, Will . . . I'll bet you that pup in there'll think twice before he ties into another big coyote."

"Me, too," said the boy quickly. "I'll know better, too. How come a coyote is so smart, anyway?"

Someone walking softly over from the direction of the house interrupted this conversation. It was Abbie, freshly scrubbed and freshly dressed, no longer wearing her split, dusty riding skirt, and with her golden hair combed to a pert prettiness.

Warfield looked and admired, and felt an

instinctive understanding how it must be for a lovely girl buried out here in this gray-dun emptiness while all her maturing instincts yearned for another way of life.

She smiled and held out two freshly baked heels of warm brown bread. Warfield and Will took them and smiled back. For a moment there was an easy comradeship here, a simple, silent acknowledge-ment of something basic that was good.

She said: "The nights aren't so bad, but the days . . . they're insufferable."

It was an easy way to open a conversation, and this was the time of day for trivial things, for a letting down of bars and barriers. Will ate on, saying nothing. Warfield leaned there, thinking.

Finally he said: "It's a big world and there are many worse places in it, Miss Abbie, even with-out the heat."

She gazed at him, faintly reproving. She was a woman with all the attributes of womankind. She didn't want this handsome, tall, bronzed older man to sound sententious. She wanted him to be light and flirtatious and fascinating. She put Warfield in mind of a thirsty man teasing him-self by shaking a half empty canteen.

Will turned suddenly and went back into the barn. He'd saved a small piece of his bread.

Warfield said: "You know what a pup is to a boy, Miss Abbie?"

She came on, leaned near him upon the rack, and shook her head. "No. What?"

"Well, first off he's a possession. Then he's a friend. Finally he's a confidant, a recipient of love a boy in his teens is ashamed to lavish on people." Warfield turned his head and smiled. "You could explain that to your pa. A boy needs a pup as much as a man needs a . . ."—Warfield almost said wife, but Abbie's slate-gray large eyes were boldly waiting, their depths full of warmth, so he shied off and ended up lamely saying—"a good horse."

She kept watching him, turning him uncomfortable with her half-girl, half-woman desires up and plain to see. "Are you going to stay hereabouts, Mister Troy?" she finally asked, her voice turning very soft.

He shook his head and fished around again for his tobacco sack. He didn't need that smoke, didn't want it, but it covered up the uneasiness stirring in him now, not entirely caused by her obvious thoughts, but caused just as much by her healthy closeness. A man much alone had thoughts that invariably turned toward women. Regardless of whatever haunting thing lived in a man's heart, he never failed to be lifted a little out of himself by the sight, the closeness, of freshness and clean beauty.

"Why not?" she asked, watching his lowered head. "There are outfits around where a man could find work, and you said yourself there are worse places on earth."

He lit up, snapped the match, and lifted his head to blow off a grayish cloud. Far off along the roof of the world a little star flashed and fell. Closer, a little breeze came downcountry laden with the scent of scorched granite, greasewood sap, and ancient dust as musty as time itself.

How did you tell a beautiful young girl it was late and she ought to go on in to bed? You didn't—you just played out the little hopeless game with her and mightily tried to avoid hurting.

"I've got a long way to go, Miss Abbie, and a strong reason for going. Someday maybe I could come back." He lowered his head. "Maybe in the spring when the desert's blooming. Before the heat starts."

She shook her head at him. "You'll never come back, Mister Troy. Do you know what kind of men head due south down across the desert from here . . . down into Mexico?"

He inhaled, closely examined the tip of his cigarette, and scowled. He knew; God also knew. And so did John Trent know.

"My father says that of every hundred who pass by in the night, fifty are outlaws running, and the other fifty are lawmen chasing them."

He turned and indulgently smiled. "And which am I, Abbie?"

"I don't know. That's what I've been trying to

56

imagine. Which *are* you?" She rose up a little and leaned closer, her arms forcing a solid roundness up near the neckline of her bodice. "It wouldn't make any difference which you are," she said, suddenly fierce. "It wouldn't make any difference, at all. But if you were the first kind . . . you'd be safe here."

He met her intensity head-on, braced into it. He smoked and gazed straight at her. He killed his smoke upon the rack, reached forth, touched her shoulders, brought her still closer, and dropped his face. Her mouth came swiftly up to him. She kissed him with a sudden fire that nearly threw Warfield off balance. And he kissed her. He needed that kiss.

He drew back, dropped his hands, and watched her eyes darken as she waited for him. "Abbie, go on in to bed. It's late." He checked himself, then said again: "Late. It's so much later than you think. Good night, Abbie." He turned and walked straight on down into the barn.

Will was there. He made a motion for silence and beckoned. Warfield went over. The pup was fitfully sleeping. Will whispered: "He ate the bread. Isn't that a good sign?"

"The best possible sign," murmured Warfield, and dropped a bronzed hand to the boy's shoulder. "You better head on to bed now, son. And, Will . . . ?"

"Yes?"

Warfield shoved out his hand. "Shake, pardner. You've got a fine pup, be good to him."

Will shook and nodded, then he said: "Good night, Mister Troy. See you in the morning."

"Sure," lied Warfield, then he turned and watched the boy walk swiftly out into the soft night, his boot steps making quick, light sounds upon the dusty earth.

Warfield went over to saddle up. The bay horse was rested and refreshed and willing. He turned without even a shake of his head as Warfield urged him on out into the empty yard, walked southward past the faintly lighted house, and kept right on walking southward. It was near midnight, which was a good time to begin a desert crossing any time of the year, but particularly in summer-time.

An orange-silver moon distantly set off the darkness and for a while Warfield could still see that house back there. Then it, too, vanished.

CHAPTER SIX

Dawn was breaking off in the hazy east when Trent met the stage hustling along through, upcountry toward Daggett. He left the road to avoid all that ensuing dust and he waved indifferently at the whip and the guard, who had waved to him first.

Not often did people envy passengers on those pitching vehicles trying to sleep and avoid being bruised by the everlasting plunging and swaying, but this morning Trent envied them. He was badly in need of sleep. Not rest, he'd gotten that back at Daggett, sitting and waiting, but sleep he hadn't gotten and now, seven miles southward, Chalmers's bitter coffee was wearing off.

He got back on the road and went along, his steeldust briskly walking through this good coolness, his thoughts bridging the years back as far as Trent's first manhunt, then jumping ahead into the elusive but probable future.

It was odd to be riding along with his thoughts drifting beyond control. He had been thinking of that first chase, wondering if that outlaw was still imprisoned or not, and the next moment he was remembering Troy Warfield as he'd been the last time Trent had seen him, remembering Warfield's crime and all the vivid impressions that killing had made upon him. Then his thoughts jumped far ahead into the predictable future and made bold pictures that could, or could not, be true. Meanwhile, the endless desert firmed up out of its nighttime shroud and turned deceptively mild and benevolent and inviting with its dawn freshness and its soft-lighted delicately molded landscape.

The stage road ran as straight as a mottled old snake. The next town was Fulton, thirty-two miles south of Daggett in the heartland of all this empty waste. Chalmers had said the only thing that kept Fulton alive was the stage line and the freighters. There was a good spring at Fulton. It was the halfway mark. Water sold for 10¢ a gallon but everything else was priced competitively.

Chalmers had had a few dry comments to make concerning Lem Bricker, who ran the town of Fulton, and one of them was that Bricker had a lucrative sideline that the strategic location of his town made possible. Even outlaws had to have water. Bricker never denied them, but there was a special rate for outlaws in Fulton—$2 a gallon.

Chalmers had said for lawmen the price remained a dime. He'd told Trent that Lem Bricker once said to him that his scheme was foolproof—if he was ever called to account, he could prove that he'd invariably helped the side of law and order by selling his water to lawmen for 10¢, while selling it for $2 to outlaws. What he'd neglected to tell Chalmers—but then he hadn't had to be this explicit—was that he knew very well lawmen couldn't afford more than 10¢ but that outlaws, fleeing with their plunder and running for their lives, not only could pay more, but would pay more.

Well, Trent thought as he fought sleep, only a fool crossed bridges before he came to them. The important thing, whether Chalmers had agreed with him or not, was that he had to arrive in Fulton before Warfield pulled out, and Warfield would hit Fulton. He had to. It was as simple as ABC. A man could not cross this desert without water.

But physical exhaustion does things to a man. Trent began to resent the quick, alert gait of his animal. He resented the growing warmth as the sun lifted above its far-away barrier. He resented the grueling ride ahead, but most of all he resented Troy Warfield.

To kill a man is not a difficult thing, providing one does not afterward make the everlasting mistake of going up to look into the face of death. Everlasting, because then a man never forgets, and the face of death is a curse that stays and stays, coming back to him in odd moments. Trent had his share of memories because when you kill a man over the width of a barroom, you can't avoid seeing his astonishment as life winks out. And Trent was human with all the frailties of humankind.

He hadn't wanted to kill that yellow-haired cowboy back in Daggett. There had been others like that one he'd avoided killing, also. But now he rode along with all the crushing weight of his own discomfort, his own suffering and deprivation, directly attributable to one man, and now he wished he could kill Warfield and get this over with. He *wanted* to kill him.

The sun climbed higher, turned a faded color, changed gradually from its earlier benignity to become a leering foe. Its scorch built up steadily making the air smell of brimstone and taste of old iron. It drove lizards and snakes and huge hairy desert spiders—tarantulas—into the panting shadeless shadows at the base of paloverdes, Joshua trees, and baking boulders.

Trent had come half the distance. Sweat made his shirt limp. He dozed off and jerked awake, doing this mile after mile. The burden of existence was almost more than a man could bear in this midday summertime desert if he was fully attuned to it, but Trent wasn't, he was traveling on guts alone. But it takes a lot more. The desert isn't a place where one ever finds excuses or compassion or pity. The desert is a world of death. It is steeped in an endless, depthless silence. In midday summertime nothing moves, nothing changes, there is neither perspective nor limit. The summer-time desert is infinity and to brace into its over-whelming immensity unprepared is fatal.

A thousand years of mankind had made only one scratch on all that changlessness—a road. And every winter the wild winds covered those roads, obliterating in a week what mankind had taken laborious generations to create. The desert never compromised.

Trent was a speck moving with painful slowness down through all that. He had his canteen but frequent injections even of the sole substance in this arid place that could prolong life were not enough. Unless a man was physically prepared in all ways, water, like the sun itself, produced not the necessary sustaining power, it produced instead illness. That's what Trent's canteen was doing to him.

He was two-thirds of the way along, the sun had begun to assume that pinkish glow from afternoon's dust-laden, metallic-scented atmosphere, when his stomach rejected water. He dis-mounted, leaned upon his horse, and gasped until the inner retching was over. Then he walked on for a mile beside the horse. That helped somewhat because he walked slowly. But in a clear moment, as he paused to look from slitted eyes out through the dancing distances, it dawned on Trent that he wasn't going to make it.

He didn't argue with this sudden, and solid,

realization. He couldn't accept it because, like all men, Trent had a secret belief in his own immortality, his own indestructability, but he also, in a very human and contradictory manner, knew that he *could* die, that someday he *would* die. But the trouble with these conflicting thoughts was simply that Trent, like most men of strength and imagination, just would not believe that this was the place.

A man should die with guns blazing, with great ideals at stake, with his courage and his convictions vindicated. He should die with glory and honor—not out in the middle of a god-forsaken desert like a rat dies or a lizard or a snake, not by simply falling down in the endless silence and yielding up his soul for nothing, so that, when he's afterward found, he's shriveled from the sun like a piece of discarded leather, burned black, and with his swollen tongue protruding making him appear in death both ridiculous and unheroic.

It was the indignation, the scorn for this kind of a death that kept Trent going. He swore at the desert, at the sun, at Troy Warfield. Even at the steeldust horse, blaming all of them for the conspiracy that had gotten him out here like this. He marched along with anger and nothing else sustaining him until three horsemen, sitting motionlessly across the roadway, gravely watching his approach, brought him to a final halt.

He peered at those burned-black desert riders. They stared back. The sun was falling away toward the west. There were thin shadows creeping out here and there across the desert's floor. One of those men was raw-boned and sparse. He had eyes as cold as the eyes of a snake; they seemed as lidless, too, because this man never blinked. On either side of him were men with more weakness, more moral frailty in their faces. But that one in the middle showed iron and unrelenting resolve.

This one finally said to Trent: "Mister, you ain't going to last long, the shape you're in. How come you didn't wait until sundown? What's your hurry, mister?"

Trent flagged outward with a stiff arm. "Get off the road," he snarled, his voice so hoarse it was barely audible. "Get out of my way." He added a fighting epithet to that, but those three horsemen sat up there, gazing downward, untouched.

"Where's his hat?" one of them quietly asked. "Look at his danged eyes . . . burned nearly closed and puffed up like he was bee-stung."

The raw-boned, leathery man in the center said nothing, but his companion to the right said: "Hell, Lem, I got my doubts about botherin' with this one. He's near done for."

But Lem knew better. "He'll make it all right. He'll be blind as a damned bat for a day or two, but this one's tough. He's mean and he's tough.

You don't see these angry ones go down on their whimpering hands and knees. Go put him on his horse, tie him up there, and let's get back."

Both the other men swung down, and, as they approached Trent, one of them said over his shoulder: "I'll look through his gatherin's." And he did that with Trent making futile, blind swings as those two manhandled him, rummaged his pockets, appropriated his wallet, his papers. Then one of them swore a strong oath and stepped away holding a bright-shining little German-steel badge on his palm.

"U.S. marshal, Lem. Look here."

Lem leaned from the saddle, took the small badge, and gazed at it for a long time. He eventually dropped it into a pocket, saying brusquely: "Hurry up, will you? We got to be back in town before evening."

They got Trent into the saddle but he still writhed and twisted, making the matter of tying him up there almost impossible, so, as Lem led the steeldust by the reins, the other two rode close on either side of Trent, balancing him up there.

After a while Trent's resistance dwindled. He sank into a kind of sick stupor. From there, all the way into the desert town of Fulton, he was like a sack of meal. They had to push him upright and keep a light hold of him, but he offered no further resistance. Finally, after something like ten or eleven hours, Trent's will had atrophied, leaving him like a vegetable—alive and functioning, but helpless and senseless.

They were within sight of the dusk-shadowed town when Lem said: "They don't send U.S. marshals after common horse thieves, boys."

One of the others agreed with this. "I never before seen one down here. I've seen deputy U.S. lawmen, sure, but not full marshals."

"Does that put you in mind of anything?" Lem asked.

The other man shrugged. "Should it?" he countered.

Lem snorted. "Yes, it should!" he exclaimed. "If you had the brains of a goat. A full-fledged U.S. marshal's after someone big . . . someone like maybe a bank robber or a big-time, stage hold-up man. Someone who's done something besides shoot a gambler or steal a horse. *Now* do you get it?"

The other rider's eyes brightened. "Sure," he retorted. "I get it. Somewhere there's a big-time outlaw and this here U.S. lawman's trailin' him. And that big-time outlaw's probably got a pair of saddlebags bulgin' with banknotes or raw gold . . . enough to patch hell a mile."

Lem smiled, swung to gaze approvingly backward, and didn't say any more because they were nearing the environs of town. He led them around to the east so that they didn't pass down

Fulton's main roadway. He obviously wished to keep Trent a secret from the rest of the town. He took them to a meandering, filthy back alley and down it to a rickety, warped horse shed and got stiffly down in front of this building, walked back to steady Trent until his companions also got down, then he walked on into the old shed.

"Fetch him in here for now," he commanded. "After full dark we'll take him into the saloon's back room." He stepped aside as his grunting companions strained on past. Trent's feet dragged lifelessly making two uneven squiggles in the dust.

They put him in a corner upon an ancient manure pile and Lem stepped up to gaze at Trent. "Sure a mess," he said. "All right, you boys stay with him. Wet some rags and put 'em over his face. Don't give him anything to drink. That's half his trouble now . . . too much water under an overheated hide. And keep him quiet. This one's ours. No one else is going to know. You understand?"

The two sweating cowboys nodded, watching Trent. One of them said: "When he comes around, he'll tell us all about that."

The other unkempt man tucked in his shirt tail and spat aside before he said: "Yeah? And supposin' this feller he's after's already rid on past? It could happen, if he started out say late yesterday afternoon. And that feller'll be smart, too. They don't put no U.S. marshals on the trail of simpletons."

"Then," said Lem in his usual, cold, hard, and thoughtful way of speaking, "we'll go after him." He looked at the other two. "We'll get him, don't you worry about that. We'll find him and I don't give a damn where he goes . . . we'll get him." Lem pointed at Trent. "But this one's the key, so you fellers baby him like he was your damned brother. I'll be inside . . . if he says anything you come tell me. Otherwise, stay with him and keep him cool until night, then we'll give him better quarters inside." Lem chuckled as he turned away. "This one's worth a fortune to us, I figure, so he deserves the best we got."

Lem stopped in the doorway, gazed outward for a moment, then said over his shoulder: "Get those damned horses out of the sun. 'Specially *his* horse." He walked on out of the shed, heading over toward the rear of a building no more than thirty feet off on his left. He entered there, looking perfectly blank and expressionless everywhere except in the eyes; there, he looked mightily pleased about something.

CHAPTER SEVEN

A man could conceivably travel through purgatory as long as he did it at night, and, barring some misadventure that might tumble him into the pit, he wouldn't suffer any noticeable inconveniences.

And the desert *was* purgatory, even at night. It fooled no seasoned traveler simply because at night it was cool and quiet and very pleasant to pass through, lacking, as it did, the mountains and cañons and other travails that beset horsemen in other places. But at night it was a pleasant kind of purgatory.

It was even a good place to dwell upon poignant thoughts, for, chameleon-like, the desert could alluringly fit a man's every mood. It could seem to smile with him, to weep with him, or it could match his melancholy. It was the latter mood it matched tonight as Warfield passed down it. Every stiff-standing Joshua tree or pitifully thin and listless paloverde seemed bowed with sadness this night. Every cactus squatting low alongside Warfield's eastward path seemed sad, seemed to understand what it was that kept the bronzed horseman's face settled in its melancholy lines.

How many times in a man's life did he find a truly receptive woman? Once, maybe twice. Not more than that, for, although the variety of humankind was endless, the virtue of selflessness was not endless. In fact, it was quite rare.

That girl back there had possessed it. She'd inherited it from her mother and it was there in her dead-level gaze, along with her need and her frustration. So, twice now Warfield had encountered the powerful constancy that makes a girl a woman, and which makes a woman loved and cherished long, long after youth departs.

That's why he rode southward down the still, warm night with his melancholy. Twice now he'd been upon the verge of true and faultless happiness, and twice now he'd had to saddle up and ride on, never to return.

It was a tantalizing thing that fate had done, permitting him two pure visions, and at the same time withholding from him the right to either.

He took a tiny sense of pleasure, though, from the knowledge of what he'd glimpsed twice, and he also thought that, sad as each departing had made him, he was still far luckier than most men, because most men never find constancy in womankind at all, fleetingly or otherwise.

And as the hours passed, Warfield's spirit brightened in another way, too. He'd suspected vaguely that by depriving his thoroughbred of rest back at Lincoln, he'd given his pursuer a near-fatal advantage. But now with the bay's great power rhythmically functioning under him, he knew this was no longer the case, and he felt good about that, so in the end, he told himself, a man's good fortunes and misfortunes balance each other out—providing, of course, that he does not make the same error twice, and providing, too, that he does not lose sight of his objective.

He came across the north-south stage road with the moon over his right shoulder. It lay there empty for as far as night gloom permitted him to see in both directions. He reined out upon it, swung southward, and let the bay have his head.

His thoughts, seldom rushing on ahead for the elemental reason that he didn't know what lay ahead, drifted back to young Will and the pup, and to the man Will longed to love but who was half a lifetime distant from the carefree toilless days of youth, and who could not breach that gap.

He thought, too, of Abbie and of Abbie's mother. He thought, finally, that he knew what he'd seen in Mrs. Crockett's expression that he hadn't been able to define, that vague regret and frustration lying just behind the smile. A mother wished for her daughter much more than life had given her. But in this desolate country—where was such a life? Nowhere. And Abbie's mother knew it. For the daughter the future held nothing grander than it had held for the mother. Work and save and scrimp—bear children, grow old, and eventually leave this same unbearably dull legacy to still another generation. If a shining knight ever came out of the sunrise or the sunset, he would come only in a dream.

Maybe someday there would be a better life, Warfield thought, but not yet and probably never in this desert world where the most Herculean efforts of the strongest men could accomplish nothing more than make a campsite that would disappear as soon as the power of sinew and muscle faltered.

He saw a milestone and read it. **Fulton—twenty miles**. He hadn't asked at the Crockett place and no one had told him there was a town down here. Not that it mattered. Nineteen miles from now he'd be interested, but right now, as every previous day—and hour—he'd lived for the here and the now. The future was inexplicably tied up with a stocky graying man astride a durable steeldust horse, and somewhere down here that other horseman was also riding. Perhaps not this late at night, yet one never knew. The John Trents of this world didn't achieve their notoriety by sleeping when other men slept or by thinking as others thought.

The bay horse shied around a mottled Gila monster in the road and walked on. The Gila monster, deadly as was his bite, was a stupid, stolid critter. He killed careless men but no other kind.

A little ground breeze came on from the north making things pleasant for as long as it lasted. This time of night it wasn't uncommon for these little whispers of fragrant air to pass along.

Warfield made a cigarette and smoked it, more to kill time than because he felt any need. In this strange, silent race for survival in which he was involved, speed was an actual detriment so far as running one's horse was concerned. Endurance mattered here—endurance, sagacity, toughness of man and horse. Perhaps a hundred miles farther south they would be neck and neck. *Then* Warfield might have to use his ace-in-the-hole. But not for a long while did he have to worry about that. At least that's what he thought.

What he had to worry about now was just exactly how long this desert was. He would stop at this village of Fulton after daybreak, and, if it was a likely place, he might even wait out the hot time of day there. According to his calculations Trent was back at Daggett. However, he hadn't gotten this far south by underestimating his enemy, either, so he would carefully assess Fulton even though he hardly thought Trent could be ahead of him.

Another of those little ground swell breezes came running along. This one came from the south and the east and it had a scent that was pungent and familiar—sheep.

Warfield wrinkled his nose. As a lifelong cowman he cared little for the odor of woollies, but he'd never been violently against sheep and sheepmen, either. In Colorado there had been enough blood shed between cowmen and sheepmen. In Warfield's experience there was enough room for both.

He speculated upon the strong scent as he rode along, and after an hour he left the stage road, following his nose. Cattle didn't thrive on the summertime desert but sheep did. In fact sheep wool seemed to act as insulation for woollies as much *against* the heat as it did against the wintertime cold. And shepherds invariably knew the land. They were more often than not an insular breed of men whose lives centered around their flock, their dogs, and the predators against whom they waged a ceaseless warfare. And shepherds had another propensity, too—they saw everything that happened within the miles-deep circum-ference of their ranging bands. Next to a saloon or a livery barn, the best place to pick up information and gossip in a new land was at a sheepherder's camp.

It was no trick to locate that camp even in the quiet depth of the night. Warfield was still a half hour's ride distant when he faintly heard the dogs tune up. He might have marveled at the sensitive noses of dogs whose lifetimes were spent in an overpowering sheep stench, but he didn't. He simply used those barks as the compass needle leading him on in.

The camp had a faggot corral laboriously built by hand enclosing nearly a full acre of dust and sand, where the woollies were enclosed at night. It also had a pair of harness mules nearly as old as Warfield was and much grayer, who solemnly walked up out of the brush, stopped side-by-side, and solemnly watched Warfield come up.

There were three long-haired dogs and one of them had startling blue eyes. These animals made the little short rushes that were typical of their kind. They weren't mean, probably wouldn't have bitten Warfield if he'd stepped down, but they were a shepherd's one-man dogs. They had a master and viewed other humans as interlopers.

The wagon was a combination Mexican *carreta* and Gypsy caravan. A crooked stovepipe protruded through an ancient and much-patched canvas top, pots and pans, along with coyote traps and other impedimenta, hung from its sides, and for a hundred feet all around the earth had been brushed off and vigorously swept clean.

Warfield sat his saddle, quietly looking. He knew those dogs had told their owner what he had to know, and that somewhere around here was a man with a gun, watching him. He spoke a little to the dogs. They listened, their tails faintly vibrated, but the voice was wrong and so was the man smell, so they stood guard in their intelligent, stiff-legged manner, until a silent silhouette stepped on around the wagon with a long-barreled Winchester rifle held up, and said gravely—"*Buenos días, hombre.*"—paused, studied Warfield a silent moment, then lowered the rifle a little, and said with a small shrug: "It is late for a person to come calling, *señor.* The night is more than half gone."

Warfield smiled. The Mexican was an old man and leathery. Once, he had been stockily compact and powerful, but a half century had passed since then. Now he was spare of build, wiry, but still heavy-boned.

"Or early," said Warfield. "It is either very late or very early."

The Mexican's teeth whitely shone. He had a great, villainous mustache that evidently was his one vanity, for it was wickedly stiff and upcurving, showing considerable care, while the rest of the old man was threadbare and colored the identical hue as the desert's ancient soil.

"You are lost, *señor*?" the old shepherd asked softly, carefully, his voice making no secret of the fact that he didn't think Warfield was lost at all.

"Not exactly. But I don't know the country."

"*Sí.* And you travel south?"

"Yes."

The old Mexican put aside his rifle, clucked at

77

the dogs to silence them, and made a gallant, old-time gesture for Warfield to dismount. "It is breakfast time, anyway," he said with the philosophical shrug of his race. "A sleepy man misses the greatest gift of God . . . a new day being born. I will stir up the fire."

Warfield got down, walked ahead, and draped his reins over a wagon wheel. As the older man went about rekindling his cooking fire, Warfield watched him, wondering what it was that made men voluntarily live this awfully lone and celibate life.

The old Mexican shook his coffee pot, found it half full, set it teetering atop some carefully arranged stones, and lifted the lid from a black, greasy pot to poke with a sage twig at the beans and mutton inside. He then reared back upon his haunches, his cape-like armless overgarment—called by the cowboys a poncho—settling upon the ground, tilted back his ancient face, and put a quiet, careful gaze upon Warfield.

He finally nodded as though to himself and said: "The night is a good time to travel, *amigo*. The darkness is a man's friend . . . along with the coolness, of course." He looked up again and smiled.

Warfield walked on over, dropped down, and said: "Tell me . . . how wide is this desert?"

The old shepherd wagged his head. "A long way yet, *vaquero*. A very long way. Perhaps a hundred miles yet, to where you are going."

"Oh? And where am I going?"

Those ancient but very clear and knowing eyes faintly widened. "To Mejíco, *amigo*, where else?"

Warfield chuckled. "And water," he said. "Where will I find it?"

"Well, first at the village of Fulton that lies in that direction," replied the shepherd, lifting an arm and rigidly pointing southeast. "And after Fulton . . . if you stay on the road, you will find another spring forty miles farther along."

"Another town?"

"No. Only a spring and a stone trough beside the road. You will find no more towns until you reach Hayfork. It is on the far edge of the desert. By then, *amigo*, you will be only one long night's ride from the border."

The Mexican's coffee started boiling. He reached over, took it off the mesquite fire, and moved the bean pot into its place. He blew on thick fingers and closely examined them, while saying: "*Vaquero*, if there was another way, I'd tell you not to ride into Fulton. It's a very bad place. Very bad. The *jefe* of that town is a man named Lem Bricker." The old shepherd looked slowly up into Warfield's face and wagged his head from side to side. "*Hombre malo, Señor* Bricker. Very bad man."

Warfield ran this through his mind. "Bad in what way?" he asked.

"He sells water, *amigo*." The old Mexican said this as though in his world there was no more deadly sin. "He gives no one a drink unless he has the money to pay for it. But that's not all. He makes men pay according to what he thinks they can afford. For you, *vaquero*, riding the back trails in the night . . . two dollars a gallon. Maybe more." At the look that came gradually to settle up around Warfield's eyes the Mexican shrugged and said: "He has *pistoleros, señor.* Too many for you to fight. Others have challenged him. They are all buried in his cemetery now . . . every one of them. I know. I've been in this desert since before that town was built. Take my advice, pay and ride on. Don't delay there."

Warfield nodded. "I'll take your advice," he said.

The Mexican smiled. "And now we eat, *amigo*."

CHAPTER EIGHT

The town of Fulton was ugly for lack of paint, ugly for lack of civic pride, and it was ugly by reason of its desolate location. And yet few towns had evoked in failing hearts such enormous relief, for even in wintertime the flat and breathless world for many miles in any direction was sere and lethal.

But with a man's needs cared for, the sum total of all that ugliness drove all but the permanent residents away from Fulton.

No one recalled how it had gotten its name, and in point of fact no one cared even though above the stage office wooden awning the name **Fulton** was painted in black bold letters, as it was also painted across Bricker's **Fulton Saloon**.

There had always been a clear, blue-water spring at Fulton. The Mexicans still called it by its ancient name: *El Ojito*—Little Eye—spring. But now there was always a solitary armed man seated nearby under Fulton's lone remaining cottonwood tree. He was Lem Bricker's toll-taker.

Bricker had taken over the town years earlier, and, excepting the few Mexican residents, no one cared about that, either. The Mexicans did nothing, which was their way. Under some circumstances they could explode, but none of those circumstances had occurred yet, and wouldn't occur until someone came along to lead the Mexicans. They inherently suffered indignities; it was in the warp of their remembering blood to be passive. Prior to the coming of the Spaniards they had been slaves to their own Indian empire for thousands of years. They accepted the yoke of domination meekly, and yet deep in their hearts they hated and resented. Still, they paid for their water like everyone else, kept their eyes upon the ground, and abided with their endless patience.

As Curly Harrison had once said, "I have a feeling about these people. They'll be dogs all right, but you can't tell when that could change overnight." Curly Harrison was the stage-line manager at Fulton.

The main vocation in Fulton was to spot strangers. It was a town where dozens of shadowy men came and went. There was no law, no town marshal, no constable, and only rarely did territorial or federal officers visit Fulton. Furthermore, its location made it an ideal place for men of the night, especially in summertime, to take their leisure. It wasn't very far from the border, and it offered everything that kind of men sought—whiskey, cards, safety from the law. All for a price.

Once, the Army had threatened to burn Fulton to the ground. That was after the assassin of a government official was discovered living there like a desert prince, harem and all. But Lem Bricker had interceded. In those days he'd just begun taking over. He'd saved the town, or so it was said, although it was very doubtful that the Army would have burned the place, and afterward he'd ruled it.

At his saloon in Fulton's central business section Bricker planned his schemes. There were several back rooms here, and sometimes his five retainers lived in them out of the general sight. Now, there were only two of Bricker's men on hand. The other three were scouting the southward passes to verify a rumor Lem had heard of a Mexican pack train of mules laden with raw gold coming by stealth into the United States where the price of gold was much higher than in Mexico.

But the two men with Lem were a pair of his toughest brushpoppers. They knew the desert and they also knew the ways of men, so, when Lem set them to rousing that used-up federal lawman, they had no trouble.

First, they cooled Trent with two buckets of tepid water poured over him. Then they got a shot glass of raw whiskey down him, and after that they sat there grinning. It didn't take long. Trent had come around finally. His eyes were swollen closed, his lips were cracked, and his face was burned nearly black, but, aside from bodily distress, tough John Trent's mind was clear.

It was after 10:00 p.m. when Lem entered the little back room, turned up the lamp, and strolled over to the cot for a study of the lawman.

"You look like the devil," he candidly told Trent. "If we hadn't found you, Marshal, believe me, you'd have been dead by now."

Trent moved weakly on the cot and tried to peer upward. He couldn't, so he said: "Who are you? Where am I?"

"You're in the town of Fulton, Marshal, and my name's Lem Bricker."

Trent tried to push upright. Lem put down a big hand restraining him. "Easy, Marshal. You couldn't stand even if you could get up. Like I just said, you're in pretty bad shape."

"Where's my horse?" Trent asked, screwing up his face in another effort to see around.

"Your horse is being cared for. He's doing fine. In fact, your horse is a heap better off than you are."

"I got to get up from here, Bricker."

Lem chuckled. Back behind him those two gunmen broadly smiled. "Not for a couple days you don't," said Lem. "It'll maybe take that long for the swelling around your eyes to go down, and until that happens, you'll be blind as a bat."

Trent dropped back down.

Bricker reached around for a chair, brought it up beside the bed, and eased down upon it. He leaned forward, saying: "Marshal, who is he? Who you after?"

Trent seemed on the verge of answering this. Then he didn't reply, saying instead: "I remember now. There were three of you blocking the road."

Lem leaned back upon his chair, the slight amusement leaving his eyes. "Marshal, I asked you a question. Who is he, and what'd he do?"

"He killed a man, Bricker, and his name's Troy Warfield."

Bricker digested this, his expression for the first time showing doubt. "Killed a man. What the hell . . . that happens every day. How come to put a full-fledged U.S. marshal on his trail? How'd he kill this man . . . during a bank robbery, maybe?"

Trent, listening to that voice, heard its brittle undertones. He wanted in the worst way to get a good look at Lem Bricker, wanted to see if the face matched the cruelty he detected in that voice.

"Speak up, Marshal. I want to know about Warfield?"

"Why do you want to know?"

Bricker turned bland. "Well, we sure don't want no killer loose in Fulton. Besides that, though, maybe we can get this Warfield for you. We've helped the law before, plenty of times."

"I'll get him," said Trent. "Friend, I've been on his trail for seven hundred miles. He's my goal. I'll get him."

"Or he'll get you, Marshal Trent. You're still a long way from Mexico. A lot of things have happened to lawmen between here and there."

Trent went silent. He explored his split lips with the tip of his tongue and put up a hand to gingerly feel the swelling around his eyes. He muttered: "That damned sun. I should've known better."

Bricker agreed. "You sure should have, Marshal, because it's beginning to look like you rode seven hundred miles for nothing. Now Warfield'll get clear of you without any sweat."

"No he won't."

"How do you know he won't, Marshal?"

"Because he let his horse get tired back at a place called Lincoln, and that let me get even with him."

"You sure he's around here?" Bricker asked, his close interest inclining him to lean forward on the chair again.

"I'm sure, Bricker. My guess is that we're traveling parallel. He could be about six hours behind me or he could be even with me. But I'll bet money he isn't ahead of me. For that matter, he could be right here in Fulton."

"Could he now?" murmured Lem Bricker, and looked around at his listening companions, and winked. "Tell me about that man he killed?"

Trent rolled his head weakly from side to side and didn't reply for a long time. Eventually he said: "You got a doctor in this town, Bricker?"

Bricker shook his head. "That's one thing we never get much call for. When we find 'em like we found you, they're usually too far gone for a sawbones to help. Otherwise, they come out of it by themselves. Anyway, there's not enough patching up to do around here to pay to keep one. About that feller this Warfield killed. . . ."

"Forget it, Bricker," said Trent. "Warfield belongs to me."

Lem's face darkened and he stood up. He considered Trent for a moment, then turned on his heel, beckoned to one of Trent's guards, and passed on out of the room with him.

The remaining outlaw said: "Marshal, it don't make no difference whether you tell us or not. We'll find Warfield. You see, don't no strangers ever ride into this town we don't know about 'em within an hour after they arrive."

"Maybe he won't come here," muttered Trent, probing the sensitive flesh of his face.

The gunman chuckled. "He'll come here. They all come here. They got to. There's no more water for forty miles, and, if they try to be cute and by-pass Fulton, we find 'em dead between here and there. This Warfield'll come here all right, don't you worry none about that."

Trent said: "I'm not worrying, friend, but you'd better start worrying if he does . . . and if you fellers try to jump him."

"Oh," said the gunman drolly. "A real hellroarer, is he? Well, Marshal, too bad you ain't got the use of your eyes, or you'd see that we aren't exactly shrinkin' violets, either . . . and there's six of us against one of him."

Trent said no more. The longer he lay there, the clearer his mind became, and, except for his face and eyes, the better he came to feel. He recalled all the guarded things Chalmers had said about this place, and Lem Bricker, back in Daggett. He also fleshed out this lean picture with what he could now figure out for himself. It didn't make him feel particularly good. Not that he worried about these men apprehending Warfield, that didn't bother him in the least. But he sensed that never before in his lengthy career had he ever visited a more completely lawless town, and, as his strength and vigor returned, he cursed the blindness that kept him helpless here.

"If he gets away this time," he said aloud, speaking more to himself than to his guard, "he'll get a forty mile lead on me, for certain. I can't lie around here for two days waiting for my sight to return."

"Well, now, Marshal," drawled that gunman over by the door, "you just ain't got no choice."

Trent muttered an oath, put out a hand, and felt the wall on his right, the cot he was lying on, and the empty space on his left where a vacated chair stood.

The gunman stood by the door, watching.

Eventually he said: "You want a drink of water?"

Trent nodded. "Yeah, and make it half whiskey."

The gunman turned, opened the door, and passed casually out of the room. Trent listened, then propped himself up and felt his hip holster. It was empty; they had taken his .45. He felt inside under his shirt. They had also found his hide-out Derringer and had also relieved him of that. Even his badge, wallet, and personal papers were gone. He lay back. Bricker was thorough. Chalmers hadn't mentioned that, but then Chalmers had never been flat on his back like this in Bricker's town, either.

Trent heard his guard coming back and waited until the man's booted feet stopped beside the bed. He then raised up, propped himself with one elbow, and held forth his hand. The gunman put a glass into it. Trent sipped, felt the sharp tang of that whiskey in the water, and went on sipping.

"Where's your pardner?" he asked the guard. "There were two of you in here before Bricker came around."

"Gone huntin'," said the gunman pleasantly. "Gone to poke around town for Warfield."

Trent finished drinking, handed back the glass, and wagged his head. "Friend, I sure hope he doesn't find Warfield."

The gunman chuckled. "Must be a powerful big reward, Marshal. Or maybe this Warfield's got his saddlebags stuffed with bank money . . . or stage-line money, eh?"

"Nope. I wasn't thinking like that, friend. I was thinking that, if your pardner jumps Warfield, you'll be going to your friend's funeral."

The guard walked back to his chair by the door.

Trent heard him put the empty glass upon a table, then drop down over there and slam the door.

"Marshal, there've been lots of hardcases come to Fulton with blood in their eye and a tied-down gun. We got quite an assortment of wood headboards over at the bone orchard. Hasn't a gunman tried this town since Lem Bricker took over."

"There could be a first time, friend, there could be a first time. But I'm not worrying too much. I don't think you boys'll find Warfield, anyway."

"Hah! You're dead wrong, Marshal. Like Lem said . . . there's water here. What he *didn't* say was that there's a guard at that well day and night and there's no other way to get a drink here than to walk right up to that spring." The guard paused to let all this sink in, then he said: "Warfield's as good as got right now, so, if I was in your boots, lawman, I'd make a deal with Lem."

"A deal?"

"Yeah. If Warfield ain't got a satchel full of bank money on him, why then he's worth a fortune in rewards. Why else would they send a full-fledged U.S. marshal seven hundred miles after him? Make a deal with Lem, split the take, and we'll deliver this Warfield feller to you when you're able to ride, tied, face down, over his saddle. You can take him back and be a big hero."

Trent lay back on his cot. He drew in a big breath and he blew it out. *Nice place, Fulton. Nice people in it, too.*

CHAPTER NINE

Evil, by its very nature, was impossible to hide. An evil man or an evil town could only thrive providing others knew it was evil. An outlaw, for example, wasn't an outlaw at all as long as he said nothing, did nothing to set others to talking.

Even a stranger in a raw land heard about evil before he ever encountered it, because evil was a topic people always mentioned. As Trent had been warned back in Daggett, so also was Troy Warfield warned at the Mexican's sheep camp.

Before he came within sighting distance of Fulton, he knew enough about the place to be wary. He didn't know the details of the place, but he knew that its character was bad, and a man who is already alert to peril around him is unlikely to ride head-on into trouble.

The place looked harmless enough to Warfield as he sat his horse a half mile out upon the desert, considering it. It looked old and sun-blasted, warped and dirty, but then so did most hastily erected trail towns he'd passed through in his lifetime.

The difference was that, here, if the stage road were suddenly to vanish, the town would die because that road was its solitary lifeline. This was not cow country by any wild stretch of the imagination. People here made their living from just one thing—that road and what it brought them, and since it was also the road into Mexico, the shadowy men who came hastily riding from the north would supply that weathered town with additional revenue.

Warfield made his long, meticulous study as an Apache would have done. He utilized all the intervening, screening desert underbrush to hide him as he rode slowly and very carefully out and around the place. He acted like a man who expected an ambush at any moment. He even left his thoroughbred hidden a half mile out, and stealthily crept up to the town, entering from the Mexican part where there were no roads, and where even the footpaths seemed casually to change and meander from day to day.

There was a grinding poverty down in the Mexican quarter, which was typical, and there were innumerable mongrel dogs that slyly watched but rarely barked as Warfield passed, shadow-like, along toward the central plaza. Here, he saw an interesting thing—a man seated lazily upon a tilted-back chair where a smoky lantern hung, facing a large well out in the dusty plaza, with a six-gun on his hip and a shotgun across his lap. Now and then, although it still lacked an hour of dawn, someone would trudge up with an *olla*, a bucket, or a pan, put a coin in that drowsing armed man's upended hat, trudge woodenly out to the well, and fill his, or her, receptacle with water, then walk gravely away.

The old shepherd's powerfully scorning denunciation rang in Warfield's ears. "He *sells* water." And: "*Hombre malo, Señor* Bricker. A very bad man!"

Warfield needed water. Not only was his canteen empty but his horse was dry, too. A very simple solution came to him where he stood, tall and motionless, between two adobe houses. That drowsing toll-taker over there on his tilted chair had evidently kept his vigil half the night. He scarcely paid any attention to the trickle of people coming forth to fill their containers.

Warfield watched the Mexicans for a while, determined from which of the little crooked pathways most of them came, and worked his way back and forth among the *jacales* until he was near that trail. Next, he studied the people. What he needed was one with a spark of resentment in his black eyes; one with a slight show of pride in the way he walked and carried his head. Someone, in short, whose second-class status did not ride easily upon his shoulders or in his heart.

But when such a person finally came padding along, it wasn't a he, at all, it was a she—a tall, handsome woman in her late twenties with her great wealth of blue-black hair caught up at the back of her head in a large bun, indicating that she was a married woman. Her jaw was roundly square and her full-lipped, heavy mouth showed a stubbornness, a solid and unrelenting pride.

Warfield stepped out, halting this woman. Her jet-black eyes sprang to his face instantly as if, even though startled, she expected him to act in a prescribed manner. There was a smoldering to those unwavering black eyes that could chill a man to the bone.

Warfield said swiftly—"*Señora.*"—and held out a limp dollar bill. "*Agua.*"

The woman looked at the bill, up at Warfield's whiskery, drawn, and burned-dark face and was as impassive as stone. The fire atrophied in her stare to be replaced with a crafty understanding.

"*Pistolero*," she murmured to him. "You are an outlaw, no?"

Warfield shrugged. "I ate with an old shepherd west of town . . . he told me this is a bad place but that there is no other water. My canteen is empty and my horse is thirsty. I will be gone southward in half an hour." He pushed the money into her hand. "*Por favor*," he murmured.

She kept studying Warfield. She was only a few inches shorter than he was, which was quite tall for a Mexican, particularly for a Mexican woman. "I know the old shepherd, *señor.* He is a good man. If he warned you. . . ." She shrugged, glanced on out through the dim predawn where a little ripple of soft Spanish was audible over at the well among the people dipping up water. "They watch," she said, evidently meaning Bricker's guards. "One cannot take too much or they come to see why." She shifted her hold on the battered wooden bucket in her fingers, closed her fingers more tightly around it. "You passed an old church coming here, *señor* . . . go bring your horse to the rear of it and wait." She walked on, her bare feet padding through the dust silently. She hadn't said she'd bring the water to the church but Warfield understood. Fear was in her. She knew something of Bricker's cruelty, obviously, and yet her pride and her resentment drove her to this.

He glided back beyond the farthest adobe hovel, circled around, found his horse, and took him cautiously down to the very edge of the town where an ancient mud cathedral stood, its walls crumbling but its bell tower showing a scant length of new rope, indicating that God may have been pushed off Fulton's main roadway, but He would not be entirely expelled from the place, and there he waited.

Off against the eastern sky a watery brightness began to show. Warfield anxiously watched this. He also listened to the waking sounds of Mexican town. A baby thinly wailed and a boy swore at an old bony cow that Warfield could dimly discern several hundred yards to the north. Two men padded past the church on sandaled feet in soft conversation, apparently heading for their work in another section of town.

A *vaquero* jogged past with his high-pommelled Mexican saddle showing little flashes of hammered silver, then the handsome woman came striding, a full bucket in both hands. Her movements were graceful despite the pull of those heavy buckets, and, when Warfield stepped up to help, she gave him a look of candid interest.

The bay horse drank one bucket dry without a pause. The second bucket he only half emptied, hesitating to smack his lips and gaze up and around, then drank on down to within four inches of the bottom. Warfield handed the woman his canteen, which she held while he poured the last of that precious liquid into it. She shook it skeptically, her head a little to one side.

"More than half," she said, and lifted her shoulders, let them drop. "From here it is a long distance to the next place. Forty miles, *señor* . . . on a half canteen." She was doubtful; it showed in her smooth expression.

Warfield took the canteen, slung it from the horn, and fished out another crumpled $1 that he put into her hand. "*Gracias, señora*, I'm grateful."

"*Por nada,*" she murmured, closely studying Warfield. "It is always so . . . they come and they ride on. *Señor*, that old shepherd you spoke of . . . he is my husband's uncle. He is old and the very old are good judges of men. I wouldn't have gotten you the water except that he liked you. *Señor*, if he hadn't liked you, he wouldn't have warned you." She put up her right hand with the forefinger extended, slowly drew that finger across her throat, and dropped the hand. "*Señor* Bricker sneers at the life of men. He has enlarged our cemetery since he came to rule this town . . . twice over. My uncle-in-law told you the truth. This is a bad town."

"Why don't you leave?" Warfield asked, held here by this woman's strong, earthy beauty and her fatalistic strength.

The woman half smiled. There was a typically Mexican fatality to that little wistful smile. Warfield got the distinct impression that this handsome woman, when she'd been a beautiful girl, had had a great many of girlhood's illusions knocked out of her.

"I was born here. My husband was born here. My little son was born here. And, *señor*, except that the land changes, where else would it be any different for us? We are Mexicans . . . no vanquished people remains with honor in their former land. You understand?"

"I understand," said Warfield. "You are very lovely and you are very wise." He turned, regret brushing lightly across his heart. He had gathered his reins, ready to mount, when she said: "There is another stranger here. They brought him in from the north road last evening, more dead than

98

alive. My husband was out gathering faggots with our burro. He saw this other one. He said he wished he could just once own a horse like this other one was riding . . . a handsome and powerful steeldust gelding."

Warfield slowly turned back, slowly loosened his hold on the reins. She was watching him with that same expression, only now the black eyes gently widened at the look that arose to Warfield's face.

"Ahh," she murmured softly. "You know this other one."

Warfield didn't respond. He stood like stone for half a minute, thinking that this *had* to be Marshal Trent, thinking that Trent *had* stolen a march on him. He looked up. "You say he was hurt?"

She made a slight gesture. "Not hurt, *señor.* Too long in the sun. My husband said this other one was out of his head when they found him. He said *Señor* Bricker himself was out there when they found this man."

"He say anything else, *señora*?"

"No," she said calmly. "Only that they will kill this one."

Warfield was surprised. "Why?"

"*Señor,*" she said in mild protest, "he had a badge. They found it. They will find out what they can from him, then he will meet with a very bad accident."

Warfield gazed at the woman. "Your uncle-in-law said it was a bad town," he murmured. "But he didn't say just how bad."

She shrugged. This seemed immaterial to her now. "You will get away now, *señor*. This other one . . . he was after you, no?"

Warfield inclined his head. "He was after me, yes."

"Then you must feel relieved."

He looked into her eyes. There was a cynicism there that he was certain hadn't been there before. It was a sort of patient cynicism, as though she were awaiting his reaction, his next words, as though she already knew what his reaction would be, and if it didn't surprise her, it wouldn't please her, either.

He swung to gaze at that eastern sky where dawn was firming up. He spoke without looking around. "I'll win my race. I'll get to Mexico now."

"And that matters most, does it not? After all, a man's life is a small thing."

He swung back expecting to see bitterness joined to her cynicism. But it wasn't there at all. Her black gaze was only darker, more unreadable than ever. He stirred where he stood. "You are my conscience, is that it, *señora*?"

"No, *caballero*, I am only a woman in this world ruled by men. I have my feelings and my thoughts, but they change nothing. This is still a man's world. You will do as you wish . . . as you think you must do."

"I will ride on."

She shrugged, holding him there with her liquid dark gaze.

"No. I will stay."

"Ahhh?" she murmured. "It is as I thought then, *señor*. It is not simply a matter of a man chasing another man."

He speculated upon her, saying quietly: "I said you were lovely . . . and wise. It seems I only scratched the surface."

"It was an obvious thing, *señor*. I knew it back there when you sent me for water. You are not a typical *pistolero*. There is between you and this other one some closeness. Some feeling. No?"

Warfield pushed back his hat, looked somberly at the brightening far-away sky, and said no more for a while. The woman continued to regard him. Around them, distantly heard, were the sounds of Fulton coming to full wakefulness.

Finally she said gently: "You are wasting valuable time. The road lies southward and the sun is coming. Within a half hour they will see you riding away."

He turned and said: "You're right, there is a closeness. If they'd let him go as soon as he's well again, I wouldn't hesitate. But to kill him. . . ."

"I promise you that, *señor*. I know these men.

101

All my people know them. I tell you honestly that they mean to kill him."

Warfield came gradually to scowl. It made a difference in him. He seemed no longer the lanky, bronzed rider he'd seemed before. He seemed now to be a deadly, very dangerous man.

"*Pistolero*," she whispered. "They are many and you are one. This is their town . . . you cannot possibly elude them for long. Whatever you do must be done quickly."

"In broad daylight?" he asked.

"No, *señor*." She turned, gazed briefly at the old cathedral, swung toward him, and said: "Go in there. Take your horse into the back courtyard where the wall is eight feet tall. Stay in there. I will help you."

He gazed at her, wonderingly. "Why?"

She made that little wistful half smile again. "Am I a Mexican to you?" she asked.

Warfield faintly shook his head. "You are a woman. A handsome, desirable woman to me."

"That is enough reason, *caballero*. A woman's heart is the same whatever else she may be. I read it in your eyes. For this little tribute from a handsome man I am grateful."

He said: "No, *señora*. That's a pretty shabby reason for risking your life."

She turned, passed along the rear courtyard wall to a sagging old postern gate made of heavy oak. She opened this gate and motioned for him to lead his horse on through.

He did, and found himself in a burial place that had been long neglected. Weeds flourished here as high as his belt.

She stood with the first golden sun rays behind her in the gateway watching him in that solemn way she had. He looked around, saw the entrance to the church on across this neglected yard, turned back, and lifted his eyebrows. She nodded at him, touched her lips with a finger, stepped out, and gently closed the oaken gate. He heard the latch drop gratingly down.

Out front, he heard riders clatter past, heard lisping Castilian and low-caste *mestizo* Mexican patois in the early cool morning, each sound bell-clear and musical. He went to an ancient stone bench and sank down. A man makes his hard decisions, usually with insufficient time for good thinking, and he afterward has his regrets.

But it wouldn't make much difference. If he'd had a full hour or a full day to decide which course to follow, he'd still have had his regrets, for that's how life is lived in a primitive world full of violence, half wise, half foolish. No one ever comes up with the correct decision, the same as no one is ever all bad or all good.

He kept thinking of the Mexican woman, kept probing that last exchange between them. He thought vaguely that it must always be that way with *any* woman. Without having a hand laid upon them, they sought tributes, sought recognition of their desirability. Whether they were married or not—but more likely if they *were* married—they needed to be reassured often that in this masculine world they were needed and important—and admired.

As for John Trent, Warfield's thoughts were less vague. As he'd told the woman, he had his reasons for not wishing Trent killed. Maybe they didn't make sense, but, after a man passes his initial youthfulness, he has his set convictions, and, right or wrong, he adheres to them.

For seven hundred miles he'd managed to elude Trent, and now, here, in this grubby, shabby desert village, it was to happen at last. They were to meet. He'd been seven hundred rugged miles seeking to avoid this meeting, and now in this wretched place everything was reversed. It made a man wonder.

CHAPTER TEN

Rest made a difference any time to an exhausted, dehydrated man, but, after sunrise with the soft light and blessed coolness coming together, a fresh vigor came from within, from deep down where some well-spring reservoir existed, making strength and a sort of daily rebirth add perspective to a man's otherwise thoughts.

That's how morning came for John Trent, silently, coolly, wonderfully, because he could see past the diminishing puffiness. Could make out the snoring guard over there with his chair propped up against the door, could distinctly see the man's gun in its sagging holster.

But a man's will recovers more swiftly than his body. When Trent raised up, he was sore in every joint and unsteady in every muscle. Stronger, yes, but still unfit.

That guard opened his eyes. He didn't move at all, he just opened his eyes and regarded Trent for a long time, then he dropped his chair down, mightily yawned, mightily stretched, and cleared his throat, spat into a corner, and said: "Well, Marshal, you're lookin' better."

"Feeling better," mumbled Trent. Then he told a

lie. "But I still can't see. You sure this goes away after a while?"

The gunman stood up, hitched at his shell belt, and kicked aside the chair. "I'm sure," he answered indifferently. "Just takes a little time is all." He reached for the latch. "I'll go see what I can rustle us for breakfast."

After the guard's departure Trent probed the swelling around his eyes, found it lessened but still there, and made a careful survey of the place where he was being held.

It was not a large room and served from time to time as a combination sitting and bedroom. Trent wryly deduced what kind of men hid out in this place, safe from sight. Then the guard returned with a bowl of mush and some black coffee. As he kicked a chair around to set these things upon it, he said: "Lem'll be in to see you directly, lawman. I'll give you a little advice in advance, too. When Lem asks a question . . . you answer it."

Trent eased up on to the edge of the bed, made a show of groping for the coffee, and sipped it. "He didn't find Warfield, did he, cowboy?"

The guard stood up, regarding Trent. Finally he said: "No. But Warfield's time has run out. He'll be found."

"He's probably already south of Fulton," said Trent. "I doubt that you'll get him."

The gunman returned to his chair by the door, sank down, and vigorously scratched his ribs.

"Lem's already sent a couple men southward. He's also sent a man northward. Don't you ever think this Warfield won't get caught, 'cause he will."

Trent finished the coffee and put aside the cup. "What does Bricker expect me to do . . . sit here and let him clean Warfield out?"

The guard smiled broadly. "You hit it plumb on the head, Marshal. That's exactly what he expects you to do, and, furthermore, that's exactly what you will do, too."

"Not when I can see, it isn't."

The gunman's voice turned a little bored with this talk. He said: "Marshal, get some sense. The only chance you got in this green world is to co-operate. Anyway, what's this Warfield to you . . . just a danged outlaw on the run. He ain't worth dyin' over."

Trent felt for his tobacco sack, found it missing, and folded his hands together in his lap. "Who said anything about dying?" he asked.

"I did, Marshal. You refuse to split the reward, or try to keep us from plundering Warfield's saddlebags, and you're going to die."

"You make it plain enough," muttered Trent, hearing a second set of booted feet approaching. He waited until the second man walked on in and closed the door, then he risked the narrowest upward peek. This other man was Lem Bricker.

As he turned back around from closing that

door, Bricker spoke. "Marshal, they tell me you're some better now. I'm glad to hear that."

Trent ignored the smoothness of Bricker's voice. He said: "No luck with Warfield, eh?"

"No, not yet," conceded Bricker, unruffled. "But we will have." He walked over and stood beside Trent on the sagging old cot. "Marshal, I'd like to take more time with you, but frankly I just can't afford to. Now listen . . . I want to know whether Warfield robbed a bank or a stage."

"Neither, Bricker. I already told you . . . he killed a man."

"Not in a hold-up?"

"No, friend, not in a hold-up. In an argument."

"Then how come them to send you instead of some lousy deputy marshal after him?"

"Because," retorted Trent quietly, "the man Warfield killed happened to be a deputy U.S. marshal."

Bricker stood a moment in thoughtful silence. He seemed to believe Trent, but this did not appear to please him particularly. He acted like a man who has just had a fond hope dashed. He said: "Where did this killing take place?"

"In a place called Shafter, up in Colorado."

"Murder?"

Trent tightened his gripping fingers. For a long while he didn't answer. "Two witnesses said it was murder, yes. And, Bricker, to puncture your little balloon about all this wealth you figure

Warfield must be carrying because a U.S. federal marshal is after him, let me explain something to you. Any time a federal officer is killed, a marshal goes after the killer . . . not a deputy marshal. As for Warfield having money on him . . . forget it."

Bricker still stood there, looking downward, his thin, long, bronzed face showing no expression. "Any reward?" he quietly asked.

"None that I know of, Bricker. Maybe the local folks up at Shafter put one up, but, as far as I know, they haven't, and, as far as the government is concerned, it never offers one for men who kill federal lawmen. You want to know why?"

"Yeah."

"Because it never has to. We always get the killers of our men."

"Always, Trent?"

"Always, Bricker."

"I wonder," mused Bricker, and turned to go back as far as the doorway. "I wonder about that."

Trent said bleakly: "You just better go on wondering. It's safer that way."

Bricker shook his head over at Trent, but all the marshal could make out through his barely slitted eyes was the blurry vision of that head wag, not the expression accompanying it, nor the look of vengeful cruelty in Bricker's eyes.

"I think I'll find out first-hand, Marshal. I think I'll use *you* as my guinea pig."

Bricker left the room, noisily slammed the

door after himself, and left Trent sitting there with some tough thoughts forming.

The guard by the door blew out a long sigh.

"Man, you just signed your own death warrant," he said resignedly. "You just give Lem all the reason he'll need to plant you in boothill."

Trent had no further comment. He sat there busily thinking. Every passing hour his strength was increasing. He knew how he must look—whisker-stubbled face, filthy, ragged clothing, face peeling, lips cracked, and his upper features swollen. He looked like a wreck; he meant to go right on with that illusion, too.

In a sudden surge of unexpected compassion his guard said: "Marshal, you should've lied to Lem. You might have stayed alive a little longer. It would've been worth it."

"Would it, friend? I think lying would come easier to you than it comes to me."

The guard shifted position and said: "All right. Have it your way. Only it's too bad you can't see the sunshine your last day above ground."

"Don't be a fool," growled Trent. "What can Bricker gain by killing me? Nothing. Nothing at all."

"Money ain't everything, Marshal. Some men got a heap of hate for lawmen in 'em. Some men steal good horses because they like good horses. Me, I got a fondness for liquor. 'Course I like money, too, but I sure like my liquor. With

110

Lem . . . he despises lawmen. That's why we got no constable in Fulton. Lem sees red just by lookin' at a badge."

"If that's true, friend," exclaimed Trent, "why then, Bricker had me tagged for a bullet when he first came on to me out there in the lousy desert!"

"He did, Marshal. He did for a fact. But he also had some notion you were after a big-time outlaw of some kind, and first off he aimed to find out all about that. But he still had in mind shooting you."

Trent eased back down upon the cot, making this appear a genuine chore. He let his breath push out raggedly and he put up a hand to his tender face. "Bricker's going to make the biggest mistake of his life, friend, when he tries killing me. I told you both . . . federal law officers take it sort of personal when someone shoots one of their own. Now I'll tell you something else . . . Lem Bricker's not in the same gun league with Troy Warfield, and even Warfield isn't getting away with it."

The gunman made a derisive snort. "Warfield," he spat out. "Who'n hell ever heard of Troy Warfield? Marshal, we got boys here in Fulton who've got reputations from here to Montana. From here to Texas and back. You think this Troy Warfield can hold a candle to these other fellers? Naw, not in a million years. Who is he anyway, some two-bit cow chaser who got gassed up on rye whiskey and gunned down a lousy deputy marshal!"

Trent let that all go by without replying to it for an interval of total silence, then very dryly murmured: "Well, I reckon you could say that of Warfield."

The guard chuckled, went to work making a smoke, and was quiet for a long time. He sat over there, idly smoking, watching Trent, and looking increasingly restless.

Time ran on. Outside, the piling up heat presaged midday. Even inside, the atmosphere got metallic-tasting and painfully dry. It was the stifling kind of heat that drove men, that made them seek escape.

The guard finally threw down his cigarette, stamped upon it, and opened the door to look out. Evidently he saw no one because Trent heard him mutter a pair of connected swear words.

Trent said from his cot: "Go ahead. Go get your drink. But fetch me back a pitcher of plain water."

The guard ignored this though, sank back down with the door remaining open, and made a circuit of his dry lips with his tongue. He was palpably beginning to resent having to sit here, was turning restless and irritable.

Trent wasn't particularly thirsty. He would have drunk water had there been any within reach, but, because his mind was not on it, was on other things entirely, he didn't push that request for water. He simply lay there, quietly resting, trying his eyes under the shielding cover of an upraised hand, and assessing his returned strength. It increased steadily as the day wore along.

He thought that by nightfall, he would be as reinvigorated as he could hope to be. He also thought that by nightfall, he would have to take the initiative. He thought it very improbable that Bricker would make any move against him in broad daylight, and of course that left the obvious alternative—murder in the night and a speedy burial.

It still seemed unreasonable for Bricker to wish him dead, and yet, as that gunman across the room had said, with some men, a badge made them see red.

It didn't matter why this was so. It only mattered that it was so. As far as John Trent was concerned, he could die in this squalid little desert village because one man here was twisted in the head concerning law officers.

But Trent had no intention at all of dying. He made a mental measurement of the distance to the door from the cot. He also struggled to recall something of the outside, but in this he failed completely. The only thing he could remember— and he couldn't recall that very well—was being taken by Bricker and those two gunmen. Beyond that he had no idea of what this town even looked like, which was a critical disadvantage.

But in Trent's favor was his supposed blindness. He thought he could dupe that guard into bringing him water. If he could accomplish that, he was confident he could also get his hands upon that man. This was his one hope, and he realized it fully, so he lay there, storing up strength and grimly playing 'possum.

CHAPTER ELEVEN

Even when a man is not in peril there is something about waiting that is unnerving. It detracts from a man's confidence, wears down his resolve, puts him almost in an importuning frame of mind.

But where there is a very real and personal danger it also puts an edge to his temper and his restlessness, which is how it worked on Warfield.

He heard the town around him, from within his walled-in hiding place. Heard people out in front of the hushed old cathedral, mingling, passing gossip back and forth, heard their footfalls and the grinding-down slowness of their wagons passing to and fro. There were horsemen, too, and he could picture them—sinewy, dark Mexican horsemen with their ornate silvered, carved Mexican saddles, almost invariably with a machete-like broad-bladed knife slung aft of the right knee. He also heard someone enter the church from around front and afterward ring the tower bell. Whoever this was, he rang that bell twice, once in the morning as though it were a call to vespers, and again in the afternoon.

He sat in cool shade with his horse wandering among the ancient tombstones, grazing. He could have closed his eyes and slept. There was a sleep-inducing peacefulness to this forgotten place. But he didn't sleep; he sat there sweating, waiting, and wondering about the impulse that had motivated him. He could have been halfway to that southern water trough by now, no more than a long night's ride from the border, but instead, after seven hundred miles, here he sat, stalled and surrounded, for a reason that no other fugitive would have considered for a moment.

The handsome Mexican woman did not return, but just ahead of the first outside shadows a tall man came quickly through the little postern gate. Warfield sat perfectly still on his corner stone bench in cloying shadows watching this stranger. He was a Mexican, perhaps thirty or thirty-five years old, and he was, like the woman, tall for his race. He wore the white cotton pants and shapeless shirt of a *mestizo* even though he possessed the stalwart leanness and the proud carriage of a *vaquero*. His features were aquiline with a high-bridged, slightly hawkish nose. There was a worried look up around his eyes even after he spotted Warfield watching him. He walked on over and stopped, looked long at Warfield without speaking, then smiled. The smile made a difference; it showed something in the man's eyes that the worry had previously obscured. This was no ordinary *mestizo*. This man had his strong pride, too, like the woman.

116

He said in flawless English: "My wife told me." This seemed in the Mexican's mind satisfactorily to establish his identity and the fact that he was a friend who could be trusted. He went on smiling at Warfield. "A person can admire courage in another, but sometimes what appears as courage is rashness. No?"

Warfield said nothing. He sat there, watching the tall Mexican and waiting for the man to say what had brought him here.

The Mexican shrugged off Warfield's careful silence and dead-level stare. "I want to know one thing before I help, *señor*. I want to know why it is that a fleeing man turns back to help the man who is chasing him."

Warfield straightened up on his stone bench, moved his right hand clear of the holstered gun on his hip, and said: "He wasn't always my enemy."

"Ahh?" The Mexican seemed to wait for Warfield to say more, but, when Warfield didn't, the Mexican made his understanding small smile again. He shifted his stance, leaned upon a massive old patio support, and said: "You know, *amigo*, it comes to a man as he grows older that it's possible to respect strength, but it's also possible to admire honor, and a man can earn respect with his gun, but he seldom earns admiration with it." When Warfield kept watching this tall Mexican, clearly forming his private opinions through their talk, the *mestizo* shrugged. "I will help," he said simply. "My wife said you were a man to be helped." He smiled a little skeptically at Warfield. "But a man doesn't always trust the judgment of a woman. Not where risking his life is concerned."

"I don't want you to risk your life," said Warfield. "All I ask is that you tell me where Bricker is holding that other stranger."

"I can tell you that, of course. But, *señor*, all I would be doing is sending you to your death. You see, Bricker's other three *pistoleros* rode back into town a little while ago, and now Bricker and his five gunmen are up at his saloon . . . where your friendly enemy is being held."

"Those three were looking for me?" asked Warfield.

"No. They went down to scout the cañons below the village of Hayfork. There was a rumor that a Mexican pack train of raw gold was coming north."

"I see. This Lem Bricker . . . he's a busy man, isn't he?"

"You have no idea *how* busy, *señor.* But there were others out hunting you. Some rode south, some rode north. I think Bricker has made your friend tell why he is here. I think, too, that Bricker believes you are worth a lot of money in rewards. That's how he operates . . . within

118

the law when it pleases him, beyond the law the balance of the time."

Warfield's picture of Lem Bricker, who he'd never seen, was rounding out into a mental portrait of a man as thoroughly evil as that old shepherd had implied. He said: "Tell me one thing, *amigo*. How do you know there were men looking for me . . . how do you know where this other stranger is being held, and how did you know that Bricker's scouts were after a bullion train?"

"It is a simple thing, *señor*. In the first place Bricker has Mexicans clean out his saloon, wash the dishes and glasses, and do all the menial work. He and his men treat Mexicans as dogs. But Mexicans are also people, *señor*."

"I see. They have ears."

"*Sí*. And the Mexicans in Fulton hate Bricker and his killers."

"How much do they hate him, *vaquero*?"

The tall Mexican made a slow, mirthless smile. "Enough," he murmured, staring straight at Warfield. "More than enough, *amigo*. Does that answer you?"

"Well, partly it does. Let me get this straight. Somehow you and your friends intend for me to start this fight for them. Is that it?"

"*Sí*. That's it."

"Why don't you start it yourselves . . . why haven't you started it long before this?"

The Mexican faintly frowned. "That's not easy to explain, but you must remember that with my people being scorned comes naturally. They will do nothing unless they have a leader they can venerate."

Warfield looked startled. "Me?" he asked.

"You," said the Mexican. "All day long we have been gathering, we have been talking and pleading and goading. This is nothing new, *señor*. It is in fact a very old hope with us. But the people would not band together and fight until someone came along who was right for leadership."

Warfield got up, looked straight and wonderingly at his companion, looked over where his horse was drowsing, and looked back again. "*Amigo*," he said, softly protesting, "I'm no revolutionary. I've never led men in battle. What you're talking about is civil insurrection. I don't know anything about it."

"But you are a *pistolero*, a gunfighter, and, *señor*, you look the part . . . you are a tall, strong man with honor and without fear . . . otherwise, you wouldn't have remained here today. This is the word I've spread among my people."

"And now they're ready?"

The Mexican inclined his head. "Ready and armed and waiting."

Warfield stood dumbfounded. He had a feeling of getting into something he knew nothing about, far over his head. It troubled him considerably. All he'd hoped for was enough aid to enable him to get Trent out of Bricker's hands alive. He hadn't thought beyond that except to have some obscure notions of afterward fleeing southward again.

But this—this was the Mexican way. It was going into battle with all the lofty ideals of warfare, and it was also on a scale of which he had never dreamed. This would be a military engagement. It wouldn't involve perhaps a dead gunman or two; it would involve the entire populace of Fulton.

He said: "I don't know. I don't think so. Listen . . . all I want is to make sure Trent doesn't get murdered. That's all. Hell, man, what you're talking about is a full-scale battle."

The Mexican pushed up off that massive adobe column. He said patiently: "*Señor*, Bricker's men have shot Mexicans down who were unarmed. They have taken our women and have made us buy back our own water. They ride us down even when they are sober. They have shot our horses, our burros, even our milk cows and our chickens in the roadways. They have completely taken over our village. Now we own nothing here and are no better than dogs. We have sent men to Daggett for help . . . the men never arrived there. We once wrote a petition to the American Army . . . two days later the man among us who could write and who had made that petition was found with his throat cut . . . and with our petition pinned to the front of his corpse."

Warfield fished around for his tobacco sack, made a smoke, offered the makings to his companion who also made a cigarette, then the pair of them lit up off the same match and stood in quiet silence, gazing at one another.

Finally Warfield nodded. "All right. But let me point something out to you. I'm already outlawed so it won't hurt me. But you . . . and your friends . . . will probably be outlaws, too, when this is over. Do you know that?"

"It has been discussed, *señor*. We know."

"And your friends are still willing?"

The Mexican nodded, saying quietly: "Being an outlaw with pride is better than being a dog without pride. They are willing."

Warfield sucked back a deep inhalation and noisily let it back out. He cast a glance skyward. The midsummer evening was descending but it would be several hours yet before nightfall. The little homely sounds of a village putting aside another day were around in the hot late afternoon, even the pungent aromas of cooking were there.

"When?" he suddenly asked.

The Mexican said, with a little twinkle: "The minute I walk out of that little gate over there, take my hat off, and mop my forehead." At Warfield's quick, wide-eyed look, the Mexican's twinkling black eyes glowed stronger. "I told you . . . we have been talking all day."

"They're out there right now?"

"All around, *señor*. Even the ones who work in Bricker's saloon have their pistols beneath their shirts. They are scattered up through the town. Some are loafing by the saloon and some are at the livery barn. There are even three men atop the stage line office roof . . . with rifles and pistols."

Warfield breathed softly: "I'll be damned."

The Mexican chuckled. "My wife wanted to come here earlier and prepare you. I thought it wiser for her not to. After all, we have a child."

Warfield put a narrowed look upon the tall Mexican. "Your people sure overlooked something," he said softly. "They're looking up to the wrong man. *You're* their leader, not I."

The Mexican's expression turned saturnine. "My people," he said slowly, "are like conquered people everywhere, *señor* . . . they are blinded by the splendor of those who have vanquished them, and see among their own kind only others as miserable as they also are. So . . . they look up to a man like you, a *gringo pistolero*. For me, the slight is nothing. I want only to be able to walk upright like a man."

Warfield smoked his cigarette down, dropped

123

it, and ground it underfoot. He was still having trouble assimilating all this. He had seen civil disturbances in his lifetime; he had even seen pitched battles. But he had never been involved in anything quite like this at all. It had nothing to do with range rights, with the wars between sheepmen and cowmen. This was purely and simply a revolution—Mexican style—and extricating John Trent from Bricker's murderous grip was going to be only a very small part of the whole thing.

He raised his head. The tall Mexican was steadily regarding him. Warfield wagged his head in a rueful manner and the Mexican smiled broadly at him. "You will do it," he said through that broad smile. "*Bueno*. Let me walk out of here and give the signal. Then you also come out."

"What's the plan?" asked Warfield.

"A very simple one, *amigo*. You and I walk up the roadway to the front of Bricker's saloon. We call on him to bring out your friend, and, of course, he won't, so then we shoot him along with his killers, take back our town, and give you back the life of your friend."

Warfield was astounded. "Pardner," he said softly, "we wouldn't be alive two minutes after we walked up there."

The Mexican dropped his smoke and stepped on it. As he raised his head, he said, as though he'd anticipated Warfield's reaction and was prepared for it: "All right, *jefe* . . . then *you* tell me."

Warfield had been jockeyed into leadership of the Mexicans. He knew it the minute his companion had spoken, even without being called chief. "We'll get under cover before we call on Bricker to turn Trent loose, and, after the shooting starts, we'll concentrate only on Bricker and his gun hands. No plundering, no general massacre. Understood?"

"Understood," said the Mexican, and offered Warfield his hand. As he shook, he said: "This *Señor* Trent . . . they are holding him in a back room at the saloon. There is always one guard with him. They mean to take him secretly out of town after dark, kill him, and bury him. I think we must attack soon now. No?"

Warfield tightly smiled. "Go give the signal," he said. "Then wait outside for me to join you."

CHAPTER TWELVE

The greatest benefit to health is the degree with which a strong man can bounce back from punishment. But even this has its limitations, as with Trent's swollen face. He had eaten twice since being brought to Fulton, had drunk sparingly, and was now, a day and a night after being brought in, as sound as ever physically. But his face still was badly blistered and puffy around the eyes.

Of course, Trent heightened this effect, too, with his cultivated deep squint, but, even without that, and although he felt fit again, he looked like a wreck. Once, one of the guards suggested that he shave and wash, but Trent declined, giving as his excuse that he couldn't see to accomplish either. The guard didn't really care, so nothing more was said about this.

Bricker came in after the last of his men had returned, reporting they could find no trace whatsoever of Warfield. Bricker was not pleased. He said with audible finality: "All right, lawman . . . we've played our little game and now it's finished. If there'd been money on Warfield, either ridin' with him or on his head, you just might've walked out of here all in one piece."

"Naw," contradicted Trent from his cot. "You never meant for it to end like that right from the start, Bricker. We both know that."

Bricker said indifferently: "Have it your way, it doesn't matter."

"I'm curious," said Trent. "What is it with you, Lem . . . what happened sometime back in your life to make you hate badges?"

"What happened, Trent? Well, it's not any one thing. It's a whole lot of things. Every time I got started at something, the law loused me up. When I was a kid first startin' out down in Texas, there was always a badge to interfere. You know what that does to an ambitious man after a while?"

"Yeah, Bricker, I know. But didn't it ever occur to you that it was *you*, not the law . . . didn't it ever cross your mind, friend, that every time you stepped outside the law to make your living, it was *you* who was wrong?"

"Wrong, Trent? What's wrong? Wrong is what folks say a man is, when he's tryin' to claw his way up the same way they did . . . when he gets caught at something they got away with. That's what wrong is. And you . . . and all the badge-heavy devils like you . . . what gives you such a high and mighty outlook? A lousy tin badge? Naw, Trent, with men like you it's the wish to look down on others. It's the desire to think

127

you're better'n anyone else . . . to have a badge and a gun to back that up with."

Trent lay there listening to that wire-tight voice getting more rabid and savage, and he thought back to hearing this kind of unstable reasoning from other outlaws and killers. Trent had a theory: when a man passed thirty he was forever molded, and, if he was a killer, he went on killing until he was himself killed. If he was a thief, he went on stealing until society took away his freedom. If he was a mad dog, as Lem Bricker clearly was, he ground down other people until, one day, they got enough and ground him down. It was John Trent's own private version of the law of retribution—with variations.

He said: "Lem, I've never known it to fail . . . a man reaches a height in his career, and his judgment is put on trial. He can turn right or he can turn left, but whichever way he turns, forever after, forges his remaining life."

"Quite a sermon," said Bricker dryly from beside the cot. "You missed your callin', Marshal. You should've been a Bible banger."

Trent ignored this. "You're at the place right now, friend. You can probably kill me . . . at least according to the numbers and the guns you can likely come a lot closer to doing it than I can come to preventing it."

"That's good reasonin'," said Bricker dryly.

"But, Lem, that's when you'll have permitted

128

your warped reasoning to turn you to the left, because, after I'm dead, you'll have made your choice, and you'll never get another full night's rest."

"Trent, you're talkin' like a fool. Who's goin' to find your grave? This is one hell of a big desert."

"I told you once, Bricker . . . federal officers make it a personal issue when one of their own is killed."

"Who'll even know you were killed? You're just goin' to disappear."

Trent shook his head. "I was last seen in Daggett. Constable Chalmers up there knew what I was doing and where I was going next. South of here on, across the desert, is a place called Hayfork. I'll never arrive there. Lem, where does that put me? Right here in Fulton!"

But Bricker wasn't disturbed. Few men in his situation were disturbed when unbalanced judgment swayed them. "Let 'em come and let 'em look," he said. "No one here's goin' to tell 'em a damned thing. And you sure won't be doin' any talkin', Marshal." Then Lem Bricker did one of the odd little things that both good men and bad men do with no really valid reason. He said: "We won't meet again until nightfall, Trent, so I'll send you in a drink . . . a double shot of rye whiskey. Even a lousy lawman deserves that before he takes off."

Then Bricker turned on his heel and walked out of the room. He paused to give a brief order to the guard at the door and afterward passed from sight.

For a little while the guard sat there, looking at Trent, his expression as indifferent as hard men have to be, then he said in a droll way: "Marshal, I got to hand it to you." He didn't enlarge upon this, he simply got up, shook his head, and walked on out of the room.

Trent opened his eyes, watched the doorway until he heard his guard and other men speaking back and forth out in the barroom, then he swung his legs over the cot's edge, stood up, and rolled his shoulders, punched at the hot, thin air with both fists, stepped right, stepped left, sat back down, and breathed deeply.

Through the grimy rear window of this room Trent could make out a dilapidated horse shed and a back alley where daylight struck bitterly against broken glass. This, he told himself, would be his way out, and if there was a horse in that shed, so much the better. If not. . . . Trent shrugged.

A noisy newcomer stamped into the yonder barroom while from the roadway came the angry cursing of someone upset by something his horse had done. A dog barked south of town and somewhere east of the main roadway a church bell pealed. This made Trent's thoughts turn ironic: *A church bell ringing in Lem Bricker's town is as incongruous as a coffin at a wedding.*

The guard returned, sauntered on in, kicked the door closed, and said: "Here's your likker, Marshal. Make it last." The man chuckled. "If you make it last long enough, it might be like a reprieve . . . no one shoots fellers while they're drinkin'."

This unfunny remark of his tickled the guard and he laughed louder as he walked ahead.

Trent had both feet planted squarely under him where he sat. He neither spoke nor raised his head, but he put out a groping hand. The gunman halted, bent slightly from the waist, and put a glass into Trent's fingers. In a blur of movement this same whiskey splashed into the man's eyes and he emitted a sharp little astonished squawk.

Trent was on his feet with both arms lashing out. The guard dropped the second shot glass and instinctively sucked back to save his middle, but Trent was after him. He caught the gunman a solid strike over the heart, struck him again in the same place, dropped lower, and sank a fist to the wrist in the gunman's soft parts. The man's breath broke past his twisted lips in a loud burst of sound, but he was tough. He would not go down. He staggered back and kept trying to get away. Neither he nor Trent was making a sound. Except for the quick, abrasive slide of their booted feet over the rough flooring, there was no noise to this battle.

Once, the gunman threw a wild right. It grazed upward alongside Trent's cheek bone and lost its force in the hair above Trent's temple. The guard then gathered himself to spring clear, and caught a short, savage blow across his left shoulder that half spun him, half threw him off balance. He didn't try to square around, he instead tried to get away, but Trent was after him with the desperation of a man who knew his own limitations. He hit the gunman again, high up alongside the jaw under the ear. He hit him again as the gunman was falling, full across the mouth. Claret spewed, the falling man's head twisted violently. He hit the floor and lay soddenly without moving.

Trent got the man's six-gun, dropped it into his own holster, stepped away, staggered, flung out an arm to steady himself, and stood there with that hand upon the wall, his head hanging, and the gasping raw sound of his own breathing loud in the stillness.

At any moment someone could walk in. Men came and went as curiosity brought them. It had been like that all through Trent's captivity and it could happen any time now—or he might be left alone for an hour. But of one thing he was quite certain, the closer it got to nighttime, the nearer drew Lem Bricker's deadline for him.

After a while he stood without support, wiped gingerly at his sweaty, raw, and swollen face, moved closer to the door, and listened. There was the usual monotone of masculine voices out in the saloon. It was getting along toward evening. Bricker's men as well as others were drifting in for relief from the desert heat. Sometimes he heard rough laughter, sometimes the call of one man to another. It all sounded casual and easy as he'd hoped it might. He looked around. His guard was lying in a little pool of red, from a broken mouth, unevenly breathing. The man would be out for some time. Trent looked back, lifted the latch carefully, and opened the door a crack.

He couldn't see into the barroom because of a partitioning wall that interfered, but on his right he could see a short run of dingy hallway. There appeared to be other doorways like his own along that corridor, all closed now, and there also seemed to be a strong silence down in that direction as though no one was about.

He opened the door wider, still couldn't see into the barroom, waited out a relishing guffaw from some bull-bass voice, then stepped through. He was now beyond any hope of consideration if he were found. By staying in the room, he wouldn't have had even this slim chance.

He looked hard down that hallway but there was nothing there, no movement and no sound, so he glided on through it, vaguely thinking there should be a rear door leading out of the building.

The corridor wasn't more than twenty-five feet long, then it abruptly swung away northward, on Trent's left. He scarcely breathed when he heard someone in a far room where the door was open. But opposite that open door was what he'd prayed he might find—a window beside another door, and the fading red light of dying day shown through that window. That second door, then, opened out into the alleyway he'd been able to see from his cot. He knew that rickety old horse shed was out there, too, which gave his spirit a surge of fresh hope.

He moved without a sound as far as that left-hand door where someone was moving, flattened there along the wall, and waited. From the sounds that unseen man was making, it seemed to Trent that this room was a kitchen, that the man in there was preparing food. He heard him rattle pans and glasses.

But the second he cast a long shadow across this kitchen opening it was sure to attract that cook's attention as Trent reached the alleyway door. He loosened the .45 in its holster, took in a big breath, and stepped boldly forward into the kitchen doorway.

Instantly, with his meager light blocked out, the cook turned his head. He had been working at a chopping block and had a large cleaver in one hand. He was a Mexican with the blackest eyes

Trent had ever seen. He stood like a statue, his face showing mild surprise but no fear or panic. In fact, Trent thought, as he leveled the .45 at this man, the Mexican's expression showed something close to annoyance.

"Put the cleaver down," Trent said.

The Mexican obeyed. He faintly scowled over at Trent. He was obviously troubled by something besides Trent's leveled pistol. Then, with his face altering to quick decisiveness, the Mexican said: "Quick, *señor*, in here. Quickly!" The Mexican whipped his head around and back again. He pointed toward a floor-to-ceiling ventilated food cooler. "Get in there."

Trent understood the Mexican's urgings all right, but he did not understand the man's sudden willingness to help him. This Mexican had not, to Trent's knowledge, ever seen him before. Certainly the man owed him no allegiance.

"*¡Pronto!*" the Mexican hissed, and dashed toward the food cooler. "*¡Señor!*" He flung back the doorway and frantically raised the screened shelves inside, making a place. "*¡Pronto!*"

Trent looked over his shoulder at that doorway leading outside. He didn't know this Mexican and he didn't trust him. Many a dead lawman had put his faith out of desperation into a fast-thinking person who had afterward sold him out.

The Mexican's face was twisted with anxiety. His black eyes were frantically beseeching. He made a furious beckoning movement with his left hand while holding the cooler's door open with his right hand. "*Señor* Trent, there is no other way for you. The others are not ready yet. Within moments now these men will discover that you are gone. You can't possibly get out of this town. There is not a chance at all for that. Now get in here!"

Trent looked at that greasy, dark, and frantic face and was puzzled. The Mexican's swift sentences had struck a responsive chord. He didn't understand, yet he felt he could somehow trust this stranger, so he put up his gun and paced over and stepped into the cooler.

CHAPTER THIRTEEN

It is the way with men, brown or white, that in times of gravity and peril, they do not show fear or worry so much as their faces reflect a stony disapproval, and if a stranger, seeing those faces for the first time, has difficulty reconciling this unpleasant regard with something else he had expected to see, it is because he doesn't understand how it is with men, usually with families and loved ones, to whom resentment and resistance mean, perhaps, also death and departure from a life, which, although it is neither pleasant nor easy for them, is still dear.

That was the impression Warfield got the moment he stepped out of the churchyard and saw those ragged, armed Mexicans standing loosely and motionlessly around there, out of sight, with their black eyes and granite faces. Their eyes moved liquidly to consider him, to run up and down him with a wooden inscrutability, while their faces showed this look of strong disapproval —not for Warfield, but rather for the thing they were sworn now to oppose with their flesh and their guns. It didn't look this way to Warfield, who had never before been part of any kind of organized insurrection, so his instant reaction was one of doubt and suspicion.

But that tall, handsome man who had been in the chuchyard spoke to the eight or ten others, and Warfield understood enough rough border Spanish to get the gist of the orders this man was giving. From here on, he told the others, he would relay orders from *Señor* Warfield who had consented to be their chieftain, and their success or their failure would depend upon the exactness with which each order was obeyed. Did the men understand this?

They did by murmuring soft assent in Spanish; they would do exactly as they were instructed.

Warfield looked at his companion, saying in English: "Is this all of them . . . what of the men you told me were around in the roadway?"

"They are as I explained," answered the Mexican. "These are only our messengers. They will carry your orders to the others."

Warfield felt relieved. "Tell them to instruct the others not to expose themselves . . . that Bricker's men are seasoned *pistoleros*."

"*Señor*," said the tall Mexican dryly, "they already know this."

"Tell them anyway, we don't want any casualties if it can be helped. Tell them to impress this upon the others. Also tell them to remain hidden while you and I go around through town to face Bricker's saloon, and, afterward, not to fire a single shot until we give the order."

These directions were quickly relayed. The messengers gravely listened, gravely nodded at Warfield, and began to glide away through the falling dusk. When the last man was gone, the tall Mexican brushed Warfield's arm with his fingers, turned, and struck off in the opposite direction. Warfield followed after, still uneasy in his mind about this thing he was committed to —this pitched battle between Fulton's inhabitants.

The tall Mexican knew every inch of ground. He took Warfield through gloomy, refuse-littered passageways between and among adobe hovels, bearing constantly toward Fulton's broad main roadway. The first glimpse Warfield caught of that avenue was from far southward where the town petered out and the desert began. Here, he led Warfield on across to the opposite part of town, into another alley, but this one was broader, then swung northward and kept walking until he and Warfield were well into the American part of town.

Up here, there was more spaciousness between buildings, and none of the adobe houses of Mexican town remained. Here, the stores and houses were of rough and badly warped lumber.

Warfield saw two Mexicans standing in shadows behind what appeared to him to be the town's livery barn. Farther along he sighted another pair of armed Mexicans at the rear of the stage office. Once, as he glanced up at the sky to estimate how much daylight remained, he spotted several dark and villainous-looking faces atop roof tops.

When his guide halted, finally, one building north of the stage office, he said softly: "Just how many men are in this with us?"

The tall Mexican carefully looked out through an opening between two buildings before he turned and said: "One can never be sure, but I think not less than fifty." He smiled, showing those large, perfect white teeth again. "Enough, *amigo*, enough." He pointed out through that gloomy runway and said: "That is Bricker's bar over there."

Warfield had already seen the black-lettered sign and knew what building he was facing. He stepped past the Mexican, paced on up through the runway, halted just short of the wooden walkway out front, and made a very careful appraisal of the town. It seemed drowsy and unsuspecting. Across the way two cowboys ambled out of the saloon to halt just short of the plank walk's edge and look right and left. One of them started to trough a wheat-straw cigarette paper and pour tobacco into it. As he did this he spoke, and so complete was the suppertime stillness of the place that Warfield heard every word.

"Wish Lem'd come up with somethin'. I'm gettin' bored hangin' around doin' nothin'."

"He will," said the other man, and spat into the roadway dust. "I learnt a year back to take it easy when I could, 'cause, when Lem says ride, pardner, you're likely to be a long time between drinks."

The smoker lit up and exhaled. He put one shoulder against an overhang post and looked dully at the town. "Too bad that Mex mule train didn't pan out. If they'd really been carryin' gold, there'd have been enough to set us all on easy street for ten years."

"He's got somethin' else on the fire."

"How do you know that?"

The second man turned toward his friend and wolfishly grinned. "I can tell. I been with him long enough to know. When he's as quiet as he is now, the wheels inside his skull are turnin'."

"Maybe," grunted the smoker. "It's probably got somethin' to do with that damned lawman in the back room." The smoker straightened up, flung down his smoke, and put a disinterested look at the pair of hip-shot horses standing under saddle at the saloon hitch rack. "Reckon I'll put up my critter," he said, and stepped down off the plank walk.

The other man said casually—"Yeah, me, too."—and headed for the other animal.

Warfield squeezed around in his dingy place and motioned for the tall Mexican to go on back out into the rear alleyway. When they were both there, he said: "Quick, into the livery barn. We want those two."

The Mexican asked no questions. He flung around and hastened toward the barn's doorless, broad rear opening. The moment he stepped inside here, Warfield heard voices on up toward the front roadway entrance. They seemed to be coming from a little room just inside the front doorway. He made the sign for silence and took the lead again, made his way carefully and silently on up to the last stall, and faded out back where heavy gloom lay with strong and pungent permanence. There, he and the tall Mexican waited.

It wasn't a very long wait. Those two gunmen came ambling on in, leading their horses. They halted and one of them made a growling call toward the little office. A man stepped out, mopping his fat, creased neck with a dirty handkerchief, threw the gunmen a look, and walked over.

A second man also emerged from that little office. He was younger, taller, and leaner than the liveryman, and didn't appear to be any part of the business. This one was armed, booted, and spurred. He seemed thoroughly familiar with the other two for he said: "Why don't you guys put up your own damned animals? You interrupted a checkers game right when I was winnin'."

Warfield drew his .45 and waited for the man in the doorway to step on out. He never did. He stood there, slouching and waiting for the liveryman to walk off with the horses, and meanwhile one of the other gunmen said to him: "Checkers? Who the hell wants to play checkers?"

The man in the doorway shrugged. "Better'n sittin' over there at the saloon doin' nothin' all day and all night." He paused, corrected himself, and said: "Not all night . . . not this night, anyway. Hey, did Lem say anythin' to you about how far out we got to take that U.S. marshal?"

The liveryman walked past Warfield without looking up. He shuffled along leading those two horses like a man to whom the eternal heat was something to be borne but which had long ago sucked out all his initiative, all his ambition and will.

Out in the runway one of those two gunmen said back to the man in the office doorway: "Naw, he didn't say, but then he don't have to draw no pictures anyway, does he?"

Warfield, waiting impatiently for that man in the doorway to step clear, finally could wait no longer. Off on his left the liveryman had turned into a pair of adjoining stalls. Any moment now he would raise his head, look around. Warfield shot his companion a look and nod, stepped forth into plain sight where he had an unimpaired view of those three men, and cocked

143

his leveled gun. Behind him, the tall Mexican stood back a little, watching the astonished liveryman.

That sound of a gun being cocked turned those three cowboys completely still. They stared at Warfield, dumbfounded.

He gave them no chance to recover. With a curt wag of his gun barrel, he said—"Into the office, all three of you."—and paced forward to be close as the gunmen obeyed.

Behind him the Mexican was gesturing for the liveryman to come along, also, but since this lethargic individual wore no gun, there was no danger.

Bricker's killers entered the office while their astonishment was still uppermost, but, once inside with Warfield standing beside the inside opening, they turned around and showed coldly calculating expressions. Their amazement was past now and gone.

The liveryman trudged past Warfield, went to a nail keg, and resignedly sank down there. He looked at Warfield from dispassionate eyes. He also studied the tall Mexican. He appeared to know the Mexican because he sadly shook his head at him, but said nothing.

"Their guns," said Warfield. "Don't cross in front of me."

The Mexican stepped around to the right, approached Bricker's men from the rear, and disarmed them one at a time. After that, he stayed back there, his gun up and steady.

That tallest gunman, the one who'd been teetering in the doorway, said suddenly: "Hey, you're that Warfield feller, ain't you?" He sounded more interested now than angry. "What the hell you think you're doing? You got the same stripe on you the rest of us got around here. Bricker'd like to see you."

"I can bet he would," responded Warfield dryly. "Now listen to me, you three, and listen good because I'm only going to say this once. Two of you stay here as hostages. One of you goes over to the saloon and tells Bricker I want Marshal Trent turned loose. Tell him, if Trent doesn't walk out of there into the roadway, I'll come over and fetch him out."

One of the gunmen who had been silent up to now put a scornful glare at Warfield and growled at him. "You fool, in the first place Lem Bricker don't take no orders from some tinhorn brushpopper. In the second place, that U.S. lawman belongs to him, and in the third place you got to be out of your damned head to think you can sneak into this town with one lousy greaser to help you, and throw your weight around."

That word greaser triggered a reaction in the tall Mexican standing behind Bricker's men. He looked past the gunmen at Warfield, slowly holstered his .45, reached forth, and lightly tapped the outlaw who'd said that on the shoulder. As this man turned, the tall Mexican dropped his right shoulder, raised up on to the balls of his feet, and swung. The sound of that blow was like a rawhide whip striking stone; it was meaty and solid and smashing. It knocked the outlaw the length of the office and dumped him half in, half out, the office doorway.

For a second no one moved or spoke, then the seated, callous liveryman shook his head dolorously again and muttered: "Vidal, that was the stupidest thing you ever done in your life . . . you with a family and all." He kept gazing stolidly at the sprawled, unconscious gunman in his doorway.

The remaining pair of Bricker's gunmen lifted their cold, reserved glances and put them gently back upon Warfield. They stood there waiting, resolved in their innermost minds what they would do to Warfield the moment this unnatural situation was reversed, but content now simply to wait. They had time on their side, they obviously thought, and would therefore use it.

The liveryman finally looked up, but he ignored Warfield and Warfield's gun. He gazed steadily at the tall Mexican. It was as though he were stolidly sad about something.

Warfield leathered his gun and nodded at that tallest gunman. There was a look to this one that

146

was uncompromisingly deadly but not vicious. For one thing he was still young.

"You go on over and tell Bricker what I said. I'll keep your friends here with me. I want Marshal Trent sent out into the roadway."

The outlaw nodded, then checked up short. "Hey," he said with sudden enthusiasm, "I think I got you figured, Warfield. You want Trent out in the roadway with a gun . . . is that it?"

Warfield was uncomprehending for a moment, but it struck him how this tall gunman was thinking, so he nodded. "Yeah, with a gun."

"Well now," said the gunfighter, beginning to slowly smile, "why in hell didn't you say that right off? I think Lem just might agree to that. You see, he wants that marshal dead, too. I think he might agree to a shoot-out."

CHAPTER FOURTEEN

Warfield went as far as the front barn entrance with the tall gunman. There, he said—"Make it good, cowboy."—and gave the gunman a little shove out into the settling evening.

For a moment he watched his impromptu messenger walking along toward the saloon with his long stride and his slight swagger. Just before the gunman passed beyond sight through the saloon's louvered doors, Warfield had a broad, boyish smile.

There was a reddish brightness to the world now. A hot and breathless stillness that invariably accompanied days' end upon the summertime desert. It was so quiet that the silence itself seemed loud. The hurting brilliance was gone but that far-out smoky haze lingered, softening the desert's cruelty and deadliness.

Warfield stood a moment, taking all this in, before he turned and paced back to the little office, stepped over the unconscious gunman, and considered their remaining captive.

"Tie him up," he said to the tall Mexican. "And the liveryman, too. Pretty quick now all hell's going to bust loose."

As the Mexican obediently went to work, none too gently, Warfield dragged the unconscious man inside and used a pair of reins to lash the man's ankles, and used his own belt to secure both arms behind his back.

He then rolled the limp body over into a corner and stood up to run sweaty palms down his trouser legs and study the liveryman, who was quietly talking to the Mexican, his voice as lacking in spirit as his eyes were.

"You can't bring it off, Vidal," the liveryman was muttering, never once looking at Warfield. "Whatever made you think you could? You and I always been sort of friends, boy, so I'm tellin' you . . . get on a horse and get out of town as fast as you can fly. They'll kill you if it's the last thing they ever do." The liveryman suddenly sat straight up and swore. "Hey, not so tight, dang it."

The Mexican finished his chore and stepped around in front of the liveryman. He was smiling. "You have your faults," he said, "but, as you said, we've been friends. That's *why* I tied you tightly, *amigo*, so you won't get loose, rush out of here, and get killed. This man and I are not alone. There are fifty more, all armed and waiting."

The liveryman's rheumy eyes widened slowly. His mouth dropped open. "Fifty . . . ?" he whispered. "Vidal, what the hell are you talkin' about?"

Vidal didn't reply. He turned toward Warfield,

still softly smiling, and there was a hard, primitive light in his black glance. It was the same glazed look of a man who has been thirsty too long and finds water, or a man who has loved not enough and who has at last found love. It was also the look of a man who has been around a long time but who has never lived. A man willing to kill or be killed.

Warfield felt solemn as a judge, but he smiled at Vidal. He understood. He walked on outside and waited in the aromatic stillness. His companion also came out. He stood listening. Then he said— "It's like the dead calm before a storm."—and ambled over closer to the roadway opening, but stood back in shadows there.

A man's strong, defiant, arrogant voice roared from across the roadway. "Hey, Warfield, come out where we can see you, and bring that Mex! Warfield, you hear me? Step out into the road."

Vidal turned his head. "Bricker," he murmured, and watched Warfield.

The silence returned and ran on, but now it was different. Now it had a sourness to it. Warfield moved up closer to the roadway and called forth, his voice sounding thin and booming where the barn's vaulted depths gave it echo. "Bricker, you got my message! You going to send Trent out or aren't you?"

"He's gone!" yelled Bricker. "He got away. He was faking. He beat hell out of one of my men and got out the back way. Listen, Warfield, step out where we can talk. I want you to help me run him down. He can't get out of town . . . I got men guardin' every path and trail. Warfield? You want to kill him, that's fine with me. But we got to team up. I know this town, but you know Trent. How about it?"

Warfield and Vidal exchanged a long look. It was clear to Warfield what the tall Mexican was thinking: *Would Warfield settle for Trent's escape, or would he continue to help the Mexicans?*

"You want to talk to me!" Warfield called back. "Come on over here to the barn, Bricker."

This silenced the other man across the roadway. With his silence the total hush of the town came down over Warfield like a solid weight. Everyone roundabout knew now something was badly wrong here, that somehow Lem Bricker had been faced up to, and the people were standing behind doors and windows, listening and waiting.

Warfield felt this. He also felt that his Mexicans were becoming restless. By now they would be stirring with their restlessness because basically brave men could stand up to death just so long.

"Bricker?"

"Yeah."

"You coming over here or not?"

"No, I'm not, Warfield. I don't like this. You're up to something."

Vidal's white teeth shone. He carefully lifted

151

his .45 and rested it over a forearm. He then raised his eyebrows. Warfield didn't nod for a long moment, not until he was satisfied he couldn't bait Bricker out of the saloon. He'd hoped to do this and avoid what was now imminent.

He nodded.

Vidal fired. Across the road a window broke and glass tinkled. A man cried out who had evidently been standing near that window, and at once a wrathful blast of ragged gunfire came back to strike the livery barn building and also to whistle down through its open and exposed gloomy runway.

Warfield threw back his head and cried out: "Let 'em have it!"

Within seconds the roadway was a deadly gauntlet of gunfire. The sound seemed to come from everywhere—from overhead, from north and south, even from around behind Bricker's saloon. It was deafening. There were pistols, carbines, even rifles and shotguns. Pieces of wood splintered under repeated impacts and the saloon's windows burst inward with a seemingly endless sound of falling glass.

From within the saloon men cried out in astonishment, in pain, and sometimes in fear. It was now very obvious that Bricker's swaggering gunmen had never considered it likely they would be involved with an army in Lem Bricker's private township. They fired back, each muzzle blast a crimson wink in the dying day, but, under the overpowering superiority of their enemies, each of those little blasts seemed almost futile, for, as soon as it appeared, a dozen answering blasts drove straight for it.

It seemed to Warfield, who was standing back there awesomely listening, that there had to be more than fifty firing Mexicans out there. It didn't seem plausible that less than a hundred guns could be making that much deafening bedlam.

From the rear of the barn a grinning, lithe, and bandoleered youth came prodding a large and paunchy man up toward Warfield and Vidal with his cocked Winchester. When he stopped close by, he yelled something over to Vidal, who turned, lowered his .45, and stared at the paunchy man, whose face was gray and whose eyes bulged. Vidal motioned for the young Mexican to take away his gun.

To Warfield, Vidal said loudly, over the roar of firearms: "This is *Señor* Harrison, who runs the stage office in Fulton."

Warfield looked without nodding. "A friend of Bricker's?" he asked.

Vidal shrugged. "Not an enemy, I think," he said, and turned back to the fighting.

Warfield stepped up and said to Harrison, who was called Curly, although he was as bald as a billiard ball: "What were you trying to do, mister . . . leave town and fetch back help for Bricker?"

Harrison vigorously shook his head. "Lord, no, stranger," he croaked. "I was trying to get away from the roadway out there. Bullets been flying through my office wall like it was paper."

Warfield looked Harrison up and down. "You got a gun?" he asked.

Harrison said that he hadn't, that he never carried firearms. He also said, rather diffidently: "What's it all about? I recognize some of those Mexicans. They live right here in Fulton. What . . . ?"

A bullet struck within six inches of where Harrison was standing. He clamped his mouth closed and gave a tremendous leap over toward the livery barn office. Then he swore eloquently and with considerable feeling. Finally he said: "Stranger, what are these men trying to do?"

"Take back their village," replied Warfield. "You object?"

"Lord, no, stranger. Nothing would please me more than to see the last of Lem Bricker and his murderers. I've been walking a tightrope ever since he came here and took over, with his killers."

Warfield jerked his head. "Go on into the office and don't come out," he ordered. "And, Harrison, don't cut loose the tied men you'll find in there."

Warfield waited until the stage manager passed out of sight, then walked up where the tall Mexican was sweating copiously and reloading.

The gunfire from Bricker's building was considerably less now than it had been. Warfield thought about this while he watched Vidal plug fresh loads into his gun. He thought Bricker's men were either hoarding ammunition or else they had been thinned down considerably. He stepped past and risked a quick look out. What he saw supported his second notion.

The building was literally being shot down, was being whittled away by that never-slackening gunfire from all over town that was being mercilessly poured into it. He stepped back as the tall Mexican finished reloading and faced Warfield, his face sweat-shiny, his eyes unnaturally bright.

"Tell them to hold up," said Warfield. "Tell them to stop firing for a while. Bricker deserves a chance."

But Vidal shook his head. "It will do no good," he said with a little shrug. "There is a difference in people, *jefe*. These men have lived with shame too long. They will not give quarter now."

Warfield frowned. This was not his way of fighting. "But Bricker's whipped," he said sharply. "By now he knows he's whipped, Vidal."

"*Señor*, being whipped is not enough. Bricker must also be *dead*."

"He may be. Now you call to those men to pass along the cease-fire order . . . or I will."

Vidal looked long at Warfield, then slowly holstered his weapon, stepped up closer to the roadway, cupped both hands, and bellowed out. He continued to shout for almost a full sixty seconds before some of that gunfire began to dwindle. When he dropped his hands and drew in a replenishing breath, he said: "I didn't think they would do it."

Actually they hadn't, for although the nearby gunfire eventually ceased altogether, farther out and over behind the saloon, other Mexicans kept right on firing into that wrecked building.

Bricker's return fire slackened off, but it took fully five more minutes before the last gun grew quiet. Then came that oppressive stillness again, that solid, pressing-down weight of insufferable silence.

Warfield heard a noise and swung around. Curly Harrison was standing in the office doorway looking owlishly out at him.

Warfield snarled: "Get back in there like I said, and keep out of sight!"

Harrison swiftly stepped back from the doorway.

Warfield moved up closer. He looked over through dust and acrid gunsmoke at Bricker's place. Even the louvered doors were gone, torn off their hinges, and lying in riddled pieces. The entire front wall was splintered, along with the windows, their sills, and even the overhead sign, which had been cut almost in two, although there had never been any point in aiming that high.

Warfield was treated to something that for him was quite new—the wholly unpredictable and wild aimlessness of Mexican wrath. It left him a little shaken.

He called out: "Hey Bricker? Answer up over there!"

There was no immediate answer, but somewhere around behind the opposite building a Mexican's taunting whistle of triumph erupted, and at once this peculiar little sound was taken up all over town, thrown back and forth for several moments, then died out.

Warfield tried again. "Bricker! This is Warfield! You haven't got much time. Answer up or you'll never get another chance."

Vidal drew in a sharp breath, and, as Warfield turned for this audible sound, the tall Mexican pointed with a rigid arm.

Across the roadway a man came out of the ruined saloon. He walked as though in a trance. It was the tall, young gunman with the boyish smile and arrogant swagger. He moved with an unnatural, mechanical step to the very edge of the splintered boardwalk, bent slightly, untied his leg thong, unbuckled his shell belt, held the thing out, and dropped it. He then stood up to his full and considerable height and said in almost a whisper: "Warfield? Warfield? Bricker can't answer you . . . he's dead. So are the others. Warfield? I surrender. I'm the only one left standin'. There are four bad hurt men over here."

Out of nowhere a solitary rifle exploded. The tall gunman's head jerked. He made a twisted grimace, turned slowly, and fell forward, face down, into the dusk-lit roadway.

Vidal jumped out into plain sight and swore fiercely in loud Spanish. From here and there other Mexicans also stepped forth. Warfield saw them all. They were sweaty and dirty and grimed with powder. Their eyes were upon Vidal as he cursed them, but, as far as Warfield could make out, there was not a solitary expression of regret for this last killing anywhere among them.

He started on across the road, halted when a short, stocky Mexican walked out of the saloon ahead of him, holding his right wrist with his left hand where blood steadily dripped, and waited. The injured Mexican came on. He looked at the others converging upon him, looked longest at Vidal, but his glance ultimately swung back to Warfield and remained there. When he was less than five feet off, this man halted and said through gritted teeth: "*Señor* Trent is in the cooler in the kitchen. I hid him there when he got away from his guard. He is unhurt, *señor*, but"— the Mexican lifted his shoulders and dropped them—"I put a little snap on the door so he cannot get out."

"You're sure he's unhurt?" asked Warfield, putting up his gun.

"I am sure, *señor*."

"Go get your arm cared for," said Warfield, and, as this older man started past in the company of other Mexicans, Warfield called after him: "*Gracias*, *amigo*, for locking him inside!"

The older man gravely nodded and walked away.

Warfield looked around and back again to Vidal. "You are satisfied?" he softly asked.

Vidal silently nodded. He was satisfied.

CHAPTER FIFTEEN

When they let out U.S. Marshal John Trent from his hiding place, he gazed owlishly at them. They filled the wrecked kitchen and overflowed out into the hallway. He could hear them speaking softly in Spanish throughout the place, but mostly from the barroom where they were surveying the awesome wreckage, and were also caring for the injured.

One tall Mexican in particular seemed in charge, so Trent concentrated his attention upon this one. He told them his name, which most of them already knew, and he explained how he'd gotten into the cooler. That tall Mexican quietly listened, seemed already to know all this, and eventually introduced himself. He told Trent he was Vidal Campos, a leader of the Mexicans. He then explained why he and his men had started their fight. He concluded by beckoning Trent along and taking him out to the ruined barroom where he showed him the bodies of three dead men, including Lem Bricker.

Curly Harrison came walking in. He seemed uncertain of himself among all those armed Mexicans. But when Harrison saw Trent gazing down at Bricker, he came over and pushed out a sweaty hand.

"I'm Curly Harrison," he said, sounding enormously relieved. "I run the stage office here in Fulton."

Trent looked from the extended hand up into Harrison's face, then past to that tall Mexican. Vidal faintly shrugged. Trent took this to mean he would not condemn Harrison or sponsor him, either, so Trent ignored the extended hand, saying: "I'm U.S. Marshal John Trent."

Harrison's mouth dropped open.

Trent critically studied the older man. Harrison was bulky without being muscular. He was bald, which made him seem older than he actually was, and he showed no sign of ever having worn a gun. In short, Curly Harrison seemed to be exactly what he was—a local townsman.

"Well, Marshal," Harrison said, "I don't know when I've been so downright glad to see anyone." He made a fluttery gesture. "The place is wrecked. My office across the road looks like someone has been firing a Gatling gun into it. This was terrible. I was sitting there, working on my books, when all at once someone started yelling, then. . . ."

Trent said dryly: "I know. I was here, too, Mister Harrison. Now tell me . . . who fired first?"

Harrison scratched his head, puckered his brow, then said: "Well, like I said, I was sitting there . . . I think it started with a blast of gunfire from here . . . from Lem's saloon."

"Were you a friend of Bricker's?"

Harrison emphatically shook his head. "Anything but a friend of his, Marshal, but we never had any trouble. You see, I paid him fifty dollars a month protection money."

Trent grew thoughtful. "The other merchants do that, too?" he asked.

Harrison nodded. "It was much cheaper than having your horses run off, your office wrecked, and maybe getting yourself dragged into an alleyway some dark night and getting half your teeth knocked out."

"Maybe," assented Trent, and stepped around Harrison, heading for Vidal who was supervising the removal of the injured gunmen. "Where are you taking these men?" he asked.

"To the women, *señor*," answered Vidal blandly, his gaze at Trent respectful but very cautious. "There is no doctor in this town."

Trent said—"I know that."—and watched the Mexicans walking out, carrying the injured. "Why did you do it, Campos?"

Vidal spread his hands. "You heard *Señor* Harrison . . . we were fired upon."

Trent put a slow, skeptical look upon the Mexican. They exchanged a long glance. Trent could not prove it had not started that way even if he'd wanted to. He knew this and so did

162

the tall Mexican. Trent gradually smiled. "You did a thorough job," he quietly said. "Lose any men?"

"Not one, *señor*, but we would have."

"Oh?"

"*Sí*. The man who wanted to keep Bricker from killing you . . . he commanded us. He told us to stay out of sight . . . not to expose ourselves. He was a smart man . . . this friend of yours."

Trent's smile faded. "A tall man," he said softly, "riding a leggy bay horse."

Vidal's expression was grave. "*Señor* Warfield," he murmured. "He hid in the churchyard waiting for dark when Bricker was to have taken you out into the desert to be killed. He waited . . . to save you from that."

"He did, did he," said Trent, reading the tall Mexican's expression plainly enough. "And in your view I owe him my life."

"As surely, *señor*, as we owe him a debt we can never repay for giving us back our town."

"Where is he now, Campos?"

Vidal shrugged and said nothing, his black eyes slowly hardening against Trent.

"Campos, he is a murderer."

Again Vidal shrugged. Some of his friends came up to stand, silent and expressionless, while listening to this exchange and watching the faces of these two.

"Marshal, sometimes a man kills with justification. Sometimes not. With *Señor* Warfield we neither know nor care. Here he showed only the belief he has that good and honest people deserve better than to be treated like animals . . . and at the same time he refused, at the risk of his life, to permit another murder to take place."

Trent looked around. All those Mexicans were closely watching him. Off to one side several others were speaking softly back and forth. These men turned and slowly ambled out of the wrecked saloon. Trent could feel the solid wall of distrust with which these men were regarding him.

He said: "Campos, Warfield is wanted by the law. My job is to bring him in. Your job as a citizen of the territory is to give me help if I need it in the performance of my duty."

Vidal's face smoothed out. He looked down his hooked nose, saying blandly: "We are a law-abiding people, *jefe*. Whatever it is that you ask, we will certainly do."

"Tell me where Warfield is right now."

Vidal waved a hand vaguely southward. "He rode away, *señor*. As soon as the fighting was over he got his horse from the churchyard and rode away."

"How long ago?"

"Not long, *señor*. Perhaps a half an hour. Do you want to catch him . . . after he has saved your life and restored order and decency to this town?"

"I'm not his judge, Campos, only a law officer who has been sent to arrest him. Of course, I want to catch him."

Vidal looked around. The other Mexicans were standing like dark statues, some leaning upon rifles, some slouching upon Lem Bricker's smashed bar, solemnly considering John Trent. "We will help you," Vidal said. "Come along."

Trent hiked on out into the darkening roadway with those silent, somber, armed Mexicans all around him. He had a bad feeling about this, but he didn't allow it to show as he went with Vidal across to the livery barn where a fat, rueful-looking man with several baggy chins was rubbing circulation back into his arms. There was another man in that little lit office, but this one was being guarded by three young Mexicans. Vidal pointed to the second man.

"He was one of Bricker's men, Marshal. He was one of the men detailed to take you out tonight into the desert and kill you."

Trent regarded that gunman, viewed the swollen lump low on the side of his face, and said: "We've met. This one was put to guarding me from time to time." Trent stepped over and stopped, the gunman sullenly watching. He said: "How about it, friend, were you to be my executioner?"

The gunman glowered and remained silent.

Behind Trent the tall Mexican stepped up to him, grinning.

The gunman said: "I was to be one of 'em, yes, but Lem never said which of us was to kill you, lawman."

"You got a jailhouse?" Trent asked Vidal. The Mexican nodded. "Then send a couple of guards down there with this man, lock him up, and hold him under guard."

As Vidal gave orders in rippling Spanish to the youthful armed Mexicans, Trent turned toward the liveryman. "You were in here when the fight started?" he asked brusquely.

"I was right here," said the liveryman dourly. "I was right here from start to finish."

"Do you know who started firing first?"

The liveryman looked over Trent's shoulder.

Vidal was standing back there faintly smiling, his dark features sardonic in the guttering lamplight. He said soothingly to the liveryman: "*Señor* Harrison said he thought the first shots came from Bricker's saloon."

Trent turned, scowling. "Let him do his own talking," he ordered.

Vidal shrugged apologetically, and kept right on smiling softly over at the liveryman.

"Well?" said Trent.

"Well," mumbled the liveryman while he massaged his arms, "I reckon that's right enough, mister. It sounded like the first volley come from over there. 'Course, you got to remember I was tied up in here and didn't actually *see* any of the actual fightin'.''

Trent turned saturnine. He was wasting time with this man. He was wasting time with them all. A very real wall of silence had settled over Fulton now. The townsmen had broken the back of Bricker's domination, which satisfied them, and it required no great powers of divination to see that from this day forward they would present a solidly unified opposition to anyone seeking to single out particular ringleaders for prosecution.

He walked out into the barn's runway and halted. There was in the back of his mind a strong doubt that prosecution should be levied against these people anyway, law or no law. But John Trent was not, as he'd said, the judge. When he got back, he'd make a full report, turn it in, and if the federal authorities thought an investigation was called for, that was their business, not his.

He ran a hand up along his scratchy, raw face. But he could do one thing. If any such demand was made, he could take over the investigation himself. This would be his only concession though. He shrugged. It would be enough. He could see that these people were justified. Had in fact been justified a long time before they finally rose up and killed Lem Bricker.

"¿Señor?"

Trent turned. Campos was standing there with those backgrounding dark and sober faces around him. It struck Trent those Mexicans were looking too bland, too solicitous.

"You are wasting valuable time, *señor*. Your fugitive is even now riding swiftly southward on across the desert."

Trent stood for a moment, gauging Campos and the other armed Mexicans. He knew as surely as he knew his own name these people, with their powerful sense of personal loyalty, would never permit him to apprehend Warfield, the man who had given them back more than their town, who had also given them back their respect as human beings. He looked away, looked down through the empty barn, caught the liveryman standing over there in his doorway gazing at him, and said: "Mister, when Bricker brought me here I was riding a steeldust gelding. Have you seen him?"

Without answering, the liveryman made a gesture toward the roadway. He seemed unable to speak, or unwilling to.

Trent turned on his heel and walked on out into the settling night. There he saw his horse saddled and bridled with several kneeling Mexicans around him making little clucking, regretful sounds. He walked on up, shouldered past, and glanced down. His horse was standing on three legs, holding a swollen foreleg up off the ground.

Trent kneeled as all the watching Mexicans became quiet. That swollen ankle was tender to the touch. Trent probed it and found something that didn't surprise him at all. Someone had pulled out a dozen tail hairs from his horse, plaited them into a strong little circlet, and had then tied them very tightly around the ankle just above the joint. Circulation had been stopped and his horse had been rendered lame.

Trent broke loose the little hair rope, stood up, and looked into those blank faces.

Vidal said: "Is it serious, *señor*?"

Trent walked back into the livery barn without answering. He collared the double-chinned owner of this establishment and said: "My horse will be lame until morning. Someone shut off his blood at the ankle. I need another horse."

The liveryman looked helpless. "Someone turned all my animals loose out on the desert a half hour ago," he said. "I'm sorry, Marshal. I can't help you."

CHAPTER SIXTEEN

The night closed in with its formless hush. Desert owls winged past, low and silent, seeking rodents. Off in the murky west a little fox yapped in his excited, swift-pealing way, and farther along a coyote rammed down to a stiff-legged halt, flung back his head, and bayed at the pale yellow moon.

The heat was gone but its strong scent lingered. Boulders yielding up their day-long store of sun blast made little brittle sounds as they cooled and the roadway smelled strongly of alkali dust. Far ahead, against the southward horizon, a peculiar soft brightness lingered above some low stark hills, and Warfield watched that light gradually die as he passed along.

Two days farther. Or a night and a day. Then he would be over the line and safe. He would make that watering trough he'd been told of perhaps by dawn, but, if he did this, it would only be because his bay horse was thoroughly rested and strong again after a full day's rest and recovery. The trough, people had told him, was forty miles below Fulton, which was a very long ride to make without a stop. On a lesser horse he couldn't even hope to make it.

He recalled the fighting back there, the things those people had said to him, the looks in their eyes and upon their faces, which were reflections of the pure things in their hearts. He thought, too, of John Trent, but he had no illusions there. You didn't know a man's unswerving dedication to duty as well as Warfield knew Trent's dedication, and believe such an unsolicited obligation as saving that man's life was going to change anything between you.

He didn't believe he'd want it that way. For a long, long way he and John Trent had been running nearly neck and neck—sometimes one leading, sometimes the other leading. After a while this grim race became more than that; it became a personal will to triumph. Not to escape for Warfield and not to make the arrest for Trent, but instead to prove by their pitted strength and their matched wits which was the better man.

It was the way of the outlaw. The chase of the hunted and the hunter. The personal involvement of their individual manhood. Now Warfield was in the lead again. He hadn't asked anyone back there to delay Trent. It would detract from his victory—if he proved victorious—to have such a thing happen. And yet there was another aspect to such a delay if it happened. It would prove that Warfield, by his unselfishness in Fulton, had earned the esteem and the prayers—and the physical assistance—of those people, so perhaps, in a way, he could say it was also part of his personal triumph if Trent were delayed to help him get safely along.

Time passed slowly as it always must when a man rides alone through the dark hours of a summertime night. And time brings its thoughts, its recollections, and its little hurting reflections.

He recalled Vidal's handsome, proud wife, and envied Vidal. He remembered Abbie's uninhibited willingness, and felt strong regret for that, too. He even remembered Derby Hat back in the town of Lincoln, and Derby Hat's panting greed. And Will Crockett with his furry pup, and the powerful love of a boy for his one true friend.

He also remembered other things, farther back in other towns, all running together to form a loose pattern that also was the way of the outlaw because every one of those things had made an impression upon his heart and his mind, exactly as his passing had left its imprint upon the hearts and minds of others.

This seemed to Warfield, as he went down the hushed night, to be the sum and substance of a man's life, this touching the lives of others and having their lives also touch him.

If there was a reason for it, it must be that good and bad are the result of chance encounters among people who are already whatever they will always be, and whatever that is, brushes off a little upon others, making them better or worse for the brief little meetings. A man without conscience for instance wouldn't have left Abbie back there with her powerful, natural hungers. He would have taken a moment of rapture first— then he would have ridden on. And ever afterward that imprint would have colored Abbie's life.

It hadn't happened like that, so Abbie still had her wistfulness, her resentment against a sere, lonely environment. But someday the man would come riding who would belong with Abbie, and then her world wouldn't be tinged with regret for the other affair and she would grow to be a better woman because there was no guilt.

And Warfield's short encounter with young Will and the pup. There, it hadn't been Warfield who had given, it had been Will. A boy's wholesome longing for affection had been strengthened by Warfield's experienced hands saving the little dog. Now that belief in the good would grow firmer in a forming lad, and conversely Warfield's own belief in the power of affection had been strengthened, also. It was very easy in this life to become cynical. But now and then a meeting with a lad and his pup kept even a man with reason for cynicism, from turning bitter and hating.

Warfield made a cigarette with his reins loose and swinging. He lit up and deeply inhaled, exhaled, and looked up into the endless mystery of the heavens. Life would end for him some-where, sometime, perhaps tomorrow or the next day. Perhaps not for many years yet. But a man's imprint lasted on through time being perpetuated in others because in even the smallest way he had touched their lives, confirming whatever it was they already were, for good or for evil, so even an outlaw on the run left his imprint in the sands of time.

He killed the smoke atop his saddle horn, dropped it into the roadway, and took in a big breath, blew it out, and watched the tailrace of a shooting star blaze down the long slope of the westerly heavens. He was a part of this night, and even after the faintest pastel brightness began to firm up off in the east, he remained a part of it, the only visible moving thing in all the desert emptiness.

Dawn came softly creeping ahead of the sunburst rush of hard yellow light, and with it came a brisk picking up of the bay's footsteps. He had caught the scent of water on ahead.

Warfield had covered his forty miles.

The trough was there beside the road exactly as he'd expected to find it. It was very old with round stones protruding from its crumbly masonry. In one corner someone had made the mark of the trinity in that worn-smooth cement. Warfield saw this and thought the old-time mission priests had erected the trough.

He drank first, then filled his canteen, and afterward off-bridled so that his horse wouldn't suck air around the bit's high-port mouthpiece and later on have an ache in his stomach.

He loitered there in the coolness, feeling refreshed and totally apart from all the rest of the world. He sighted a small desert deer coming along, her large ears up and moving, her small feet delicately, warily lifting and falling. Then she saw the bay horse and in a twinkling was gone again. Warfield smiled and got back astride, turned southward, and passed downcountry again.

The sun jumped up an hour later, flooding the desert world with its fierce, golden brightness. Within another hour Warfield heard a stage coming and left the road, sat far out, watching as that rocking, plunging vehicle with its driver, its guard, and its four straining horses raced by.

Afterward he went along with the dusty smell of roiled air accompanying him until he saw his first tree. It was a silvery-barked old cottonwood twisted and turned from wintertime's buffetings, its leaves green on top and pewter-colored underneath.

He watched that tree for a long time, until he was abreast of it, and then he felt the softer sponginess of loam, instead of gritty sand, under his horse as he gradually left the desert behind, passing now into a less astringent world where a steady coolness from green places ameliorated that increasing heat.

It was near 10:00 a.m. by the sun's position

when he sighted the town. Although he had never been here before he knew its name—Hayfork. Like a great many names in this raw world, Hayfork had its connotations for Warfield. Even if he'd come here in the darkness, he still would have thought this was a farming-ranching country. In the desert country names ran from Gila to Blue Water to Apache Pass to Purgatory, but in greener places the names were more like Meadowland or Tanque Verde—or Hayfork.

The air was like clean glass, which made Hayfork appear two miles closer than it really was. But those two miles gave a stranger all the time he needed to make his appraisals, his adjustments, and his decisions.

Hayfork lay beside a willow-lined creek that ran east and west. It was the usual scattering of buildings hugging a central, congested area where stores stood shoulder to shoulder.

There were trees around Hayfork, which was not usual in this part of the West, as well as what was obviously the remains of the customary old-time plaza. All borderland towns had these plazas. In the old days Spanish soldiers had been quartered here to protect people from marauding Indians. Now, those ancient plazas served more pleasant purposes. The customary dug well was there for people to get water. The ankle-deep dust was there, also, waiting to burst upward under the impact of booted feet making little puffs that hung in the still air.

Hayfork had less of the raw newness Fulton had possessed. It seemed not only much older, but much more peaceful, which was what Warfield was looking for as he approached the place.

There were the saloons, the variety houses where men gambled and danced. There was even a bank, indicating that law and order as well as thrifty prosperity existed here. And there was a low-roofed forbidding, thick-walled old adobe building in the center of town with the nearly illegible lettering across its upper front stating that this was Hayfork's *calabozo*—jailhouse.

Warfield passed two outbound freighters with ten mules to each rig and a bronzed driver sitting high up with his swamper upon the spring-set seat. They waved and he courteously waved back.

It was good to be in a place where a man could greet others without wondering about their motives. He reined over to head down the main roadway, his decision made.

He would lie over here all day if he could, before tackling that last forty miles, but he would also keep close watch upon the northward roadway that was visible from almost every part of town, because sooner or later, he very well knew, Marshal Trent would come swinging along.

At the livery barn an old man steadily puffing a corncob pipe from his tipped back position upon a chair closed his whittling knife with a positive snap and looked quietly upward as Warfield turned in. He removed the pipe, looked northward up into the visible desert, spat, and said drawlingly: "Hell of a country on women and horses."

Warfield stepped down, slapped alkali dust off his pants with his hat, and smiled. "Not too good on men, either."

The old man soberly nodded, jerking his thumb backward toward the barn. "The day man's inside. He'll take care of your critter."

As Warfield struck out through the doorway, the old man's frosty glance stayed upon him.

Across the way was a fairly good painting upon a saloon's front wall of a tall glass of beer with an inviting ring of foam atop it. Warfield was drawn over there by that wordless suggestion, while behind him the old man with the corncob pipe kept watching.

The saloon was gloomy and all but deserted. A bartender leaned disconsolately upon his high counter with his chin resting upon one cupped hand. His eyes picked up Warfield at the door and studied him all the way across the room. Without a word the barman turned his broad back, drew a glass of beer, turned back, and wordlessly set it on the bar before his solitary customer. Warfield dropped a small coin, upended the glass, and drank it down.

As he handed over the glass for a refill, the

barman said conversationally: "It's that sign out there. The second I see a stranger with trail dust on him come through that door . . . I know exactly what's on his mind."

Warfield took the second glass but held it upon the bar top. He glanced around. Over in a dingy corner sat the only other patron of the place—an old man exaggeratedly scowling at a newspaper in his hands while he held it to the light forming each word with his lips as he laboriously read.

"Pretty quiet yet," said the barman, seeing Warfield's glance around. "Things don't get goin' in Hayfork much before evenin'. But after that, there'll be poker and monte, if you feel like waitin'."

Warfield said: "Mister, I feel like a bath, not a card game."

"Sure. Two doors south at the first intersection. There's a tonsorial parlor around there. For a dollar they'll shear you, shave you, and shine you. For two bits they'll give you two buckets, show you the pump out back, and let you use the tub room." The barman shook his head. "Hell of a price ain't it . . . two bits for a lousy bath and a man has to pack his own water."

"Not to me," said Warfield, drinking down that second glass of beer. "It'll be worth five times that much to me just to *see* that much water." He pushed back the glass, nodded, and started back out of the saloon.

As Warfield hit the walkway outside, he caught the hat-shadowed leathery old face of the man across the road in front of the livery barn upon him. He turned and started along toward the first intersecting roadway.

CHAPTER SEVENTEEN

The alternatives for John Trent were simple. He could lie over in Fulton until morning and possibly his lamed horse would be capable of traveling by then, and, if so, then Trent could head for Hayfork via the old water trough in the blast-furnace heat of the day.

But if his steeldust wasn't ready for the trail by morning, then Trent would have wasted an entire night, and also would have to wait out the night and leave the following morning, and this, he thought as he ate a greasy meal at Fulton's only café, would be giving Warfield all the advantage.

Trent tossed off the dregs of his second cup of coffee, paid up, and strolled back out into the shadows. Across the way he saw several men spiritedly talking in front of the stage office. One of them was Agent Harrison but he didn't recognize the others. Around him, Fulton seemed pretty much as it had seemed before, except that the hitch rack in front of Bricker's place was significantly empty of tied saddle horses, and the saloon was unlit.

There were a few other noticeable differences, too, but since Trent did not know this town, had never seen it before the battle, they went unnoticed by him. For one thing, there were Mexicans strolling the hot night up along the business section. For another thing the merchants and townsmen seemed relieved, seemed willing to remain out after dark, and over at the livery barn two men sat on tilted-back chairs out front where they could catch the slightest breeze if one happened along. One of these was the liveryman himself and the other was that tall Mexican, Vidal Campos, who had looked Trent straight in the eye and told him, without ever opening his mouth, and yet as plainly as a man could be told, that if he went after Warfield, Fulton's Mexicans would make a point of seeing to it that he never caught Warfield.

Well, that was over now. They had purposefully lamed his horse, Warfield was a long way southward, and Trent was standing there, feeling well fed and lazily at peace—at least he felt this way physically. But in his mind was the fretful knowledge that, although he'd briefly held the advantage over Warfield and had been so sure how this was all going to end, now fate had set him afoot and the fugitive was gone again.

Curly Harrison saw Trent and broke off from his friends to walk over. Trent watched him come without feeling anything for the stage-line agent one way or another. Harrison was, in Trent's view, one of those innumerable folks in this world who sincerely wanted good law enforcement like they wanted good government, but shrank from doing anything toward achieving either.

Harrison stepped up onto the sidewalk, smiled, and said: "Marshal, I been thinking. With your horse lame and all, you can't get along about your duties, can you?"

Trent gave the obvious answer, but he gave it dryly and almost sarcastically. "That's right, Mister Harrison, I'm afoot. Did you have some remedy for this in mind?"

"Yes," said Harrison firmly, and Trent turned to gaze straight at him. "You see there's a special stage due in shortly, and it'll only be here long enough to change horses, then it'll head south for the bank down at Hayfork."

"I see," murmured Trent, beginning to feel revived hope. "And I can ride it down there."

"Well," explained Harrison, beginning to fidget and qualify himself, "actually, no passengers are supposed to be aboard this particular coach, Marshal. You see, it's a bullion shipment from the Denver Mint to the bank down at Hayfork. But I was thinking . . . if the special guards could be talked into making a special allowance in your case. . . ."

"When'll this coach be along, Mister Harrison?"

"Any minute now," replied the stage-line agent, and swung automatically to squint northward through the gloom. "It had a half hour layover at Daggett, so's the men could eat and the teams could be changed. Then it left town for here."

Trent got to thinking. He said: "Mister Harrison, do you suppose Lem Bricker knew about this money shipment?"

Harrison wagged his head and looked worried. "No. I've done this before, Marshal. Kept it a strict secret, I mean. If I hadn't . . . well . . . you know what would have happened."

"That was risky, Mister Harrison. Do you also know what Bricker'd have done to you if he'd ever gotten wind that you were smuggling large shipments of money right through his town under his nose?"

Harrison nodded, his troubled expression deepening. "I know. Yes, indeed, I know. And it's made a nervous wreck of me, too. That was one reason I was so greatly relieved when Bricker and his band were broken." Harrison ran a handkerchief up over his bald head, mopping at perspiration. He rolled his eyes around and brought them back to Marshal Trent. "By the way," he said, dropping his voice, "there is quite a little feeling building up against you, Marshal. The Mexicans . . . and not just them, either . . . say you'll be a heartless ingrate if you go after this Warfield feller after all he's done here for the town . . . and for you."

Trent rummaged for his tobacco sack, remembered that one of Bricker's men had appropriated it, and dropped his hands as he said: "I know all that, Harrison. I'll take my chances." Trent cocked his head.

The distant sound of a heavy vehicle careening southward down the northward night came faintly to him. Harrison also heard this. He swiftly looked around. That sound firmed up in the still night.

"Come on," said Trent, and stepped down into the roadway on his way across to the stage office. "Where'll they switch teams?"

Harrison hurried along, saying swiftly: "I'll show you. We have a holding yard around back."

Trent let the station agent lead him through to the stable and vehicle area behind his office. Here, a Mexican youth with a bucket of axle grease and the applicator—which was a large wooden paddle—stepped up and smiled. Trent recognized this one. He'd been a battler in the earlier fight, but right now he didn't look formidable at all.

Another Mexican was readying two teams of large, sleek horses. He looked up, gave Trent a wooden nod, and said to Harrison: "It is coming?"

Harrison nodded and passed back toward the rear doorway into his office. Here, in black shadows, he waited until Trent paused beside him, then, sounding nervous, Harrison said: "Marshal, I won't know these special guards.

There'll be two of them. I'll talk to them, but actually they aren't under my authority at all."

Trent, listening to the coach enter Fulton from the north, said nothing back to Harrison. He wasn't concerned with the guards one bit; he was concerned about those Mexicans out there. They'd be watching him narrowly, and, if he moved to enter the coach, they just might make some move to prevent that.

The coach and four came beating along with increasing noise, swung wide into the rear yard, and drew down to a grating halt. At once the driver called out and flung off his lines, set the brake, and began to clamber down.

The Mexican team master rushed up to take the horses off the pole so that he could hitch the fresh animals to the rig, and the youthful, grinning younger Mexican paddled up on his sandaled feet to inspect and grease the running gear.

Two men alighted from the coach, one getting down from the left-hand door, the other alighting from the right-hand door. Both these men carried shotguns along with their belted six-guns.

Harrison cleared his throat and fidgeted.

Trent strolled out to the nearest of those two armed guards, quietly introduced himself, and showed the badge he'd retrieved from Lem Bricker's body. The guard grounded his riot gun, considered the badge, turned, and whistled for his companion to step over, then the pair of them listened stoically as Trent spoke, relating everything that had happened in Fulton this day.

One of the guards looked around, saw Harrison, and beckoned him over. He asked the agent some questions, obviously with the intention of matching Harrison's answers with Trent's statements. Afterward he said to Trent: "You know, Marshal, I always had you figured for a much bigger man."

Harrison, evidently thinking there was skepticism in this, said hastily: "Oh, I can vouch for him being Marshal John Trent, all right."

"Yeah?" said that same tall guard, putting a slow look upon Harrison. "How? You know him personally?"

"No, not exactly. But before I was transferred down here, you see, I was assistant freight agent up at Denver. I've seen Marshal John Trent many times, although we never knew each other, you understand." Harrison nodded firmly. "This is Marshal Trent and he's on the trail of an outlaw just like he said, gentlemen, and he's got to reach Hayfork."

This tall guard looked at his companion and shrugged. "All right with me," he said, "if it's all right with you."

The second man was less suspicious, anyway. He said smoothly: "Sure. Anyway, he'll ride inside with us." With this veiled threat both the guards nodded at Trent.

The Mexican team master finished hitching up and sang out to the driver who was impatiently straightening out his new lines atop the high coach seat.

The driver looked around and down, bobbed his head at the guards, and kicked off the foot brake. Trent swung to look out over the yard. Both those Mexicans were standing stonily there, watching him.

As the coach began to move, Trent swung up behind the guards who were already taking their seats, and called out, saying: "*Adiós, amigos* . . . tell Campos I make him a present of my steeldust horse!"

The coach swung around and lurched out into the ghostly roadway. With a whistle, a pop of his whip, and a flick of the lines, the driver set his course due south and let the horses have their heads.

Trent sat down and hung on for the first quarter mile, until the coach's pitching began to assume a rhythmic swaying, then he gradually relaxed. And he smiled. Not because he was now probably going to overtake Warfield, although this pleased him, too, but because of something he'd done on the spur of the moment that made him feel better.

He didn't hold it against those Mexicans back there for what they had tried so hard to do. He admired them for that. In Trent's rough life he'd met very few men who would actually risk their own happiness to help another man. And Trent knew how it was with people like those Mexicans. He'd ridden this Southwestern land enough in his travels to appreciate just how grinding their poverty invariably was. But they were great horsemen. It was their heritage and it came as much from Anáhuac as from Castile. The steel-dust horse would put Vidal Campos in a position where a proud horseman ought to be—atop an animal he could be proud of.

Trent chided himself a little for that spontaneous gesture, but he continued to smile faintly, too. He thought that perhaps of all the sudden decisions he had made in his lifetime, this one was the best. It showed a man who was opposed to Trent, that there was warmth, understanding, and perhaps even sympathy behind the marshal's badge.

One of the guards lit a terrible cigar and quietly smoked as he studied Trent. The other guard yawned and let his shotgun lie lightly under his hands upon his lap. This one said: "Tell me, Marshal, what's this feller done you're after?"

"He killed a man," replied Trent over the endless rattling and squeaking of the coach.

"Down here?"

"In Denver."

"Well, was it a shoot-out or was it murder?"

"Murder, friend. If it'd been a shoot-out, I

wouldn't have chased him near eight hundred miles."

The guard said no more. He looked out the window, watching the desert rush rearward. His companion removed the stogie, examined its crinkly ash, flicked it, and said: "Marshal, this feller you're after wouldn't be Troy Warfield, would it?"

Trent's eyes ran over to this man. "It would," he said. "You must be from up around Denver to have heard."

The guard went on studying his cigar, his expression smoothly thoughtful. "Laramie," he said. "But we got newspapers in Wyoming, too."

Trent kept watching this one because it was obvious the man would say more and Trent was braced. He knew what the guard would say.

"I don't know, Marshal," the man finally drawled, lifting his eyes. "There is killing . . . and there is killing."

"You're lucky," said Trent sharply, "to be able to judge men. I can't. My job is to bring them in."

The guard kept studying Trent, his face gravely considering. "Everybody judges," he said quietly. "There is that thing in the Bible about 'judge not lest ye be judged.' Well, I'm forty-three years old and that means I've lived just long enough to begin to see that there's a lot in life that just don't add up. People judge

190

other people every day of their lives. They appraise 'em and they judge 'em, and, by golly, it's as natural as eating and sleeping. You may not think you do it, Marshal, but you do."

"Do I?" Trent asked coldly.

"Sure you do. You're doing it right now. You're chasing Warfield because you've judged him guilty under the law. If you catch him, you'll return him to Denver because you figure he's got it coming . . . whatever the law does to him for that murder . . . and if that's not judging a man, I don't know what is."

Trent looked for a long time at that guard. He couldn't even remember the man's name, although back in the stage yard he'd introduced himself, but something about this man disturbed Trent. He didn't know whether it was the cold look or the accusing words, but it disturbed him anyway, so he said no more and looked away.

CHAPTER EIGHTEEN

After full daylight had thoroughly firmed up, an unusual coolness came out of the breezy west and among Hayfork's inveterate loafers—such as that old man with the corncob pipe at the livery barn—this caused some comment and some quickening interest.

Rainstorms were rare upon the desert in midsummer but they were far from unheard of. Sometimes two or three years would pass without a cloud appearing out of the west. Then again a cooling breeze might suddenly start blowing, some dirty old gray cloud banks might build up, and within a few hours there could be a deluge. Just as unpredictably, too, those clouds might float over and dump their water fifty miles away. One never knew, but that didn't keep Hayfork's citizens from speculating.

Warfield was freshly bathed, freshly fed, and smoking serenely upon a roadside bench beneath a tree with his hat tipped forward when he first sensed the change in Hayfork and felt that unexpected coolness against his sunburned skin. He pushed back his hat, looked at the sky, saw those far-away drifting dark clouds, and watched them, while around behind him on the opposite side of the tree, but upon the same bench, two old men fell to discussing the probability of a midsummer cloudburst,

Warfield listened, shortly decided that the old men didn't actually know any more than he, a stranger, did, and sat on with his long legs thrust out, with that blessedly cool breeze pushing against him, and smoked his cigarette to its end.

He was sleepy, not physically tired particularly, just sleepy. He'd napped there on that bench for two hours, or until the little cool wind had awakened him, but he was still sleepy.

Some cowboys loped into town looking pleased. Even their horses seemed to have lost their summertime lethargy now as that wind increased a little, scuffing dust banners out in the roadway. People emerged from stores to scan the sky, turn, and comment to other people.

Warfield watched and softly grinned. Hayfork had a creek and trees and green fields out beyond town. It wasn't nearly as hot as the northward desert had been, and yet Hayfork's inhabitants seemed relieved at the prospect of a good cooling rain.

He got up and strolled over to the livery barn to look in on his horse. The old gaffer perched atop his tipped-back chair was still puffing and whittling. He nodded and Warfield nodded back.

Warfield's thoroughbred was filled up and drowsily standing over a manger of clover hay he hadn't been able to make much of a dent in. The coolness with its rainy taste and fragrance filled the barn, too.

The daytime hostler walked up, halted, and leaned heavily upon a wire rake.

"Maybe we're in for a little storm," he said, eyeing the bay horse. "Sure hope so. Gets so after a while a feller just ain't got no energy, these hot summer days."

Warfield turned, saying politely: "Yeah. If it hits that northward road, the thing'll turn into a quagmire."

"Right," agreed the hostler indifferently. "That road's got no bottom to it. When it gets bad in wintertime, the coaches sometimes can't make it."

This mention of stages suddenly struck Warfield. He said sharply: "Any coaches due in here this morning?"

The hostler shook his head. "Not till evening. This time o' year the stage-line folks try to schedule their runs for dawn and evening. Too hard on horses otherwise, crossing that lousy desert."

Warfield's little sudden fear faded away. He sniffed the breeze and looked around. "Anyone care if I flopped down in a stall and took a nap?" he asked.

The hostler said: "Naw. I only wish old Grandpaw Mike would go on home and smoke his danged corncob and do his whittling so's I could crawl into the hay, too." The hostler drew himself up to move off. "Take any stall on the left-hand side, mister. I just finished putting in fresh bedding."

The hostler ambled on up toward the roadway and Warfield waited a moment, watching him, before he turned and started to head for one of those shadowy, cool, and inviting horse stalls.

But as Warfield was moving, a paunchy, short man, wearing a vest with a massive gold watch chain, came briskly into the barn and called out in a sharp, authoritative way to the hostler.

"Augie, there'll be a coach in directly from Fulton. Get ready for it."

Warfield saw the hostler's expression turn from its customary heavy, stolid look into a slow grimace of indignation.

"What coach?" demanded the hostler, sounding nettled. "There ain't no coaches due in here until tonight and you dang' well know it, Josh."

The man called Josh puffed up at this insolence. "You do as you're told," he growled right back. "There's a special coach comin' in and you need to get stalls ready for the horses and be ready to show 'em where to park the rig."

Augie leaned upon his rake, studied the paunchy man a moment, then said: "All right. No point in getting huffy, Josh. What kind of a special coach?"

But Josh was turning back toward the roadway. All he said was: "Never you mind what kind of a special coach. Just see that you're ready when it gets here."

Warfield stood back without moving. A special stage from Fulton meant only one thing to him. Somehow—how wasn't important—John Trent had managed to leave Fulton, and, in a manner that was much faster than a saddle horse would have been, was now coming to Hayfork.

The livery-barn hostler came trudging along, mumbling to himself, still carrying his steel rake.

Warfield said: "Saddle my horse for me, I'm heading out."

The hostler stopped dead still and looked at Warfield. It was obvious what he was thinking. Here was a man who'd just complained of being sleepy, so sleepy in fact, he was willing to bed down in a horse stall. And now all of a sudden he was wide awake and itching to ride off. The hostler dropped his eyes, straightened his mouth, turned, and started for Warfield's horse more disgruntled than ever. Perhaps, had he been less phlegmatic, he'd have had some doubts, some suspicions, but he clearly didn't have, although Warfield watched for signs of wonderment.

While he stood there in the breezy runway carefully speculating, it came over Warfield that he probably didn't have much time. If that coach had left Fulton last night, then it must be nearing Hayfork right this minute. He went over and helped the hostler, turned his horse once, stepped up over leather, hooked both booted feet into the buckets, and flipped the man a silver dollar.

"Keep the change," he said, and rode out of the barn's runway, leaving the hostler with the first glimmer of pleasantness he'd had upon his face all day.

At the roadway that old man with the corncob pipe paused at his whittling to look up, nod very slightly, and jerk his knife-holding right hand southward. "Not quite forty miles straight on south," he said distinctly around the pipe. "Good road all the way. You'll see a pile of stones with a bronze plaque on it . . . that's the border. Good luck."

Warfield stared at the old man, stared at his leathery face and his long, faded eyes. "Thanks," he murmured.

The old man's lips softly smiled. "Don't mention it, cowboy," he quietly said. "I come this way once myself. But that was almost a half century ago. Still and all, I never felt comfortable gettin' any farther north o' the line than this here town." The old man looked down, resumed his pointless whittling, and puffed on his pipe.

Warfield rode on out, turned right, and passed

down through Hayfork, feeling a little regret. He had planned on a longer rest. As he cleared the town's farthest environs, he philosophically told himself it didn't matter. He'd rest in Mexico. Rest for a year, maybe. The main thing was that his thoroughbred was rested and strong.

Once, some distance along, he turned and looked back. He thought he saw a banner of dust standing above Hayfork's main thoroughfare but couldn't be sure. If it was dust, that probably meant the stage had arrived back there.

Still, he didn't worry. There were creek willows off on his left, indicating that Hayfork's little meandering creek ran through this southward country, too, and, moreover, he'd distinctly heard it said that no stages ran during the heat of the day. So his heretofore most pressing problems were no longer problems at all.

He rode until high noon, then halted in a bosque of trees, ate his last can of sardines, had a quiet smoke, and didn't see a thing up the long length of that northward roadway. The little breeze that had cooled the town was not running this far south, so it was hot, but not nearly as hot as it had been back on the desert. Down here, from time to time, he saw windmills and green fields and fat cattle. He also saw an occasional ranch house, but all this pastoral scenery only relaxed him the more.

He rode along through the warm afternoon,

drowsing fitfully from time to time, letting all the tensions of this grueling chase gradually go out, leaving him loose and easy. He figured he'd hit the border around midnight, or a little after.

The hours slipped by, afternoon came with its soft smokiness, and later on dusk began to settle. Once, about 5:00 p.m., Warfield moved off the road to allow a stage to race past, but after that, although he saw ample fresh horse sign as he passed along, he never once encountered another rider.

Night came with its velvety softness. He stopped once at a tin trough to water his horse. Here, the cattle smell was very strong. Here, too, stood a squeakily revolving windmill and off on his left several miles away was a house that he could only make out by its golden-lit windows where a man sat comfortably with his family unaware of the sadness that dragged at Warfield out in the night, as he passed silently by looking at those little squares of good light.

Near midnight he saw more lights, but these flickered from time to time, indicating that they were made by lanterns. He felt the rise of the old wariness at that sight and reined away from the road, but it never once occurred to him that those men down there might be anything but camping travelers or perhaps men out looking for a lost horse, a strayed child, or perhaps night-lighting deer hunters.

Not until he was a good half mile east and within sight of what appeared to be a conical-shaped monument of some kind, did Warfield decide those men were blocking the southward roadway over the line into Mexico. That monument he felt certain was that marker the old man back at Hayfork had told him about. He was well away from it now, on this eastward tangent, but he could see into Mexico beyond that mythical line where those men had their roadblock established.

He kept watching those lanterns out there. They seemed no more than the flicker of fireflies as he progressed steadily southeastward, and, as this distance widened, he thought those men had to be both stupid and careless to have lanterns at a roadblock.

Then he found out they were neither stupid *nor* careless.

Ahead, a man's even drawl came up out of the night accompanied by the sharp click of a gun being cocked.

"Hold it, stranger, right where you are!"

The bay horse, as startled as Warfield was, stopped suddenly without any restraining hand to encourage him in this, his little ears pointing dead ahead, his body stiffly motionless.

Three men strolled up. One from straight on. This one had a cocked Winchester in his hands. The other two came up from either side, very efficiently closing Warfield in, and they also had guns in their hands.

Warfield knew instinctively that somehow Marshal Trent was behind this. He could not right then imagine how Trent had accomplished it, and so great was his sudden let-down that he didn't try to puzzle it out. He just sat there, dumbly gazing at his captors. Less than a thousand feet away lay Mexico!

"Get down, mister," said that cowboy with the Winchester. "Nothing funny now . . . you'd only get killed. You see, those fellers over there with the lanterns are listenin'. They know you're down here, too."

Warfield swung stiffly to the ground.

The closest man put away his six-gun and peered closely into Warfield's face. As he did this, one of the others said: "The stage'll be along pretty quick, Sam, don't worry about it. If we got the wrong one, he can ride on." This same man considered Warfield's horse and shook his head. "Bay thoroughbred. This here's the man all right." He stepped up a little. "Is your name Warfield?"

The numbness of defeat so close to victory left Warfield disinclined to say a word, so he only half-heartedly nodded.

The cowboy slowly grinned. "Ever hear of signalin' with mirrors, Warfield?" he asked. "That's how we got you. Picked up the signals from town this afternoon. Seems a U.S. federal marshal's after you."

Warfield had his answer to how Trent had worked it. Heliograph signals. He fished out his tobacco sack and went to work. As he lit up, one of his captors mumbled something to the others and walked away to the west. Warfield thought this one was going over to tell the men at the fake roadblock Warfield had done exactly as they'd tricked him into doing, and had been captured. He snapped the match and gazed onward over that little intervening distance into Mexico. So near, and yet so far. He swung to gaze at his captors.

"What else did the heliograph tell you besides my name?" he asked.

"That Marshal Trent wants you for murder."

Warfield exhaled and gently nodded. "Did it tell you how that murder happened?"

His two remaining captors shook their heads, their faces interested. They were typical cowboys of the Southwest, hard, brave, but fair men, and, more often than not, sympathetic men.

"I shot a man who was unarmed in a saloon. Only I didn't know he was unarmed."

"Yeah?"

"Yeah. And the reason I shot him . . . he said something about Marshal Trent's wife that was a filthy thing to say, and which was a pure lie."

The cowboys exchanged a look and one of

them shrugged. "What's so terrible about that?" he asked.

"It was murder," said Warfield simply. "Would you like to hear what makes it so ironic?"

"Sure."

"Marshal Trent's wife is my sister."

The cowboys looked surprised, then bothered about something. One of them said: "Hell, Warfield, are you tryin' to tell us this here Marshal Trent's after you for somethin' like *that?*"

Warfield didn't answer the question. He shoved a hand deep into his trouser pocket, saying: "I was a deputy U.S. marshal. So was the man I shot. That makes a lot of difference." He drew forth his hand and held it out, palm up. There was a little silver badge lying there with Warfield's name engraved upon it.

The range riders peered at that badge and slowly looked up again. They had nothing to say for a moment, then one of them put up his .45 and mildly swore as he looked at his companion, saying roughly: "I won't be a part of anything as lousy as this."

The other man scratched his head and was slower coming to his decision. He said: "Warfield, you lyin' to us?"

Warfield handed this man the badge. "Keep it," he said. "Give it to Marshal Trent when he gets here. I'll be standing beside my horse just beyond that monument yonder. I won't run.

When Trent gets here, ask him. If I was lyin' . . . blaze away."

Warfield took up his reins and started walking. He didn't walk fast but neither did he look around, and when he stepped over into Mexico, he did exactly as he'd said he'd do. He stopped by the international marker and waited.

A half hour later Trent arrived with three armed deputy sheriffs in a stage. Warfield still stood there. Trent saw him, saw the marker, too, and when he walked on over, all those range riders converged, asking questions. Trent brushed them aside, went right up to the U.S. side of the marker, and put a long, steady stare upon his brother-in-law. Then Trent pushed out his right hand.

"You win," he said. "For your sake I'm glad, Troy."

Warfield shook and dropped Trent's hand. He softly smiled. "A feller does a lot of thinking on a ride like this, John," he said. "Someday I'll come back, then we can sit down and talk."

"I'd like that," said Trent, and stepped away as Warfield turned, swung up, and rode slowly down through the darkness deeper into Mexico.

ABOUT THE AUTHOR

Lauran Paine who, under his own name and various pseudonyms has written over a thousand books, was born in Duluth, Minnesota. His family moved to California when he was at a young age and his apprenticeship as a Western writer came about through the years he spent in the livestock trade, rodeos, and even motion pictures where he served as an extra because of his expert horsemanship in several films starring movie cowboy Johnny Mack Brown. In the late 1930s, Paine trapped wild horses in northern Arizona and even, for a time, worked as a professional farrier. Paine came to know the Old West through the eyes of many who had been born in the previous century, and he learned that Western life had been very different from the way it was portrayed on the screen. "I knew men who had killed other men," he later recalled. "But they were the exceptions. Prior to and during the Depression, people were just too busy eking out an existence to indulge in Saturday-night brawls." He served in the U.S. Navy in the Second World War and began writing for Western pulp magazines following his discharge. It is interesting to note that all of his earliest novels (written under his own name and the pseudonym Mark Carrel) were published in the British market and he soon had as strong a following in that country as in the United States. Paine's Western fiction is characterized by strong plots, authenticity, an apparently effortless ability to construct situation and character, and a preference for building his stories upon a solid foundation of historical fact. *Adobe Empire* (1956), one of his best novels, is a fictionalized account of the last twenty years in the life of trader William Bent and, in an off-trail way, has a melancholy, bittersweet texture that is not easily forgotten. In later novels like *The White Bird* (1997) and *Cache Cañon* (1998), he showed that the special magic and power of his stories and characters had only matured along with his basic themes of changing times, changing attitudes, learning from experience, respecting Nature, and the yearning for a simpler, more moderate way of life.

Center Point Large Print
600 Brooks Road / PO Box 1
Thorndike ME 04986-0001 USA

(207) 568-3717

US & Canada:
1 800 929-9108
www.centerpointlargeprint.com